Dallas

Called to Return

By

Ronna M. Bacon

Call to Me, and I will answer you, and show you great and mighty things, which you do not know." – Jeremiah 33:3, NKJV

In my distress I called to the LORD; I cried to my God for help. From his temple he heard my voice; my cry came before him, into his ears." – Psalm 18:6, NIV

Table of Contents

Chapter 1

Shaking the large flakes of snow from his jacket, Dallas Chisholm stepped into the kitchen of the aunt and uncle of his friend, Breck Curran. He had been at loose ends that Sunday afternoon and Breck and his wife, Neasa, had tracked him down. It was early December, and a light snow was falling. A Christmas snow, his own mother would have called it. He greeted Bonnie, his friend's mother, and slipped off his shoes, setting them neatly to the side before he hung his jacket on a peg.

Breck looked around, his eyes narrowing. He sensed something was up and not sure what. Neasa had disappeared towards the family room where she heard voices and music.

"Mom?" Breck turned to his mother, watching Dallas as he did so.

"What?" Bonnie looked innocent as she turned away, to finish fixing the trays of sandwiches that she had been working on.

"Mom?" Breck turned as he heard a female voice and listened before his face lit up. "She's home?"

"She is. Barnabas, Aubrey, and his folks are here." She watched as he rushed from the room before she turned to Dallas. "Go on through, Dallas. You know the way."

"I do. Can I do anything for you?"

Bonnie shook her head. "No. Go and enjoy yourself." She watched as he walked away, a prayer raising for her young friend. She sensed that he was unsettled.

Dallas watched as Breck hugged the young lady who was standing behind his father, who was seated at the baby grand piano. He sensed the happiness that he felt. Neasa wrapped an arm around him, hugging him.

"You haven't met Deri yet."

"No, I don't think I have." He hugged Aubrey, Barnabas' wife. "She's been away, hasn't she?"

"She has been for almost ten years now, only home once in a while." Neasa watched as Breck greeted his father, his Uncle Brock, his Aunt Beth, and his cousin, Devin. "Breck, Barnabas, and Deri were good friends through school, all part of the same crowd. I knew her slightly from the church youth group. Devin was there as well. But those three? They were the ones who came up with all the fun that we had. They were the leaders in the group."

"They still are." Aubrey drew in a breath. "Oh! They're going to sing! Wonderful!"

"Sing?" Dallas stared at her before he stared at the group. "Oh! I didn't know that they did."

"They used to do the worship team at church until Deri moved. That kind of broke up the group. Dad and Uncle Brock are still involved as is Devin, but both Breck and Barnabas stepped back. I asked Breck why once. He said his heart wasn't in it anymore and he looked sad. I think it was because Deri was missing."

"It was." Aubrey looked over at Neasa. "He told me that one day just after he had talked with her. He's been worried about her and doesn't know why."

"I find it strange that she's come home. Mom said it was for good this time. Aunt Beth hasn't said much, she indicated." Neasa had taken to calling her in-laws Mom and Dad.

"No? Hmmm. We'll need to find out. We can still pray for her." Aubrey looked up at Dallas. "Dallas?"

He came back to the present, smiling down at Aubrey. "It's okay, Aubrey. Just a walk down memory lane at the tune." He turned his attention to the group, listening to Beck on the piano, Brock on the drums, and Devin on the saxophone. He wasn't sure what Beth was playing and finally realized it was a viola.

The group broke up at last, Breck heading for Neasa, an arm around Deri.

"She's home, Neasa!"

"So I see. Welcome home, cuz." Neasa hugged her before she turned to Dallas.

"Dallas, this is Breck's cousin, Deri."

Deri looked up at the tall man who stood in front of her, taking in the thick blond hair cut just a little longer than would be expected and the deep gray eyes. Her heart stopped for a moment before a hand was held out for him to shake.

"Hi. Nice to meet you."

Dallas took in the red-gold curls that fell just below Deri's chin and the amber eyes with flecks of brown, blue and jade, and fell for her in just one look. She's the one, isn't she, Lord?

"You as well. Welcome home." He pointed to the couch. "Have a seat? And can I get you anything?" He stopped. "I'm asking that in your own home, aren't I?"

Deri laughed. "It's okay. I still feel like I am visiting, even though I have been back for three days. It's what I would do, you know? Come home once a year for a week and then fly back to where I was living." She took the plate he handed her and browsed the food, choosing only what she knew she would eat.

Dallas watched her as they ate, sitting beside her. He frowned for a moment. There was something going on he decided, reaching for her plate as she finished and stacking it with his on an end table.

Pulling out her phone that kept vibrating, Deri sighed. They just won't leave me alone. I told them that I was moving home. For their protection and for mine. She stared at the text before with a strangled sob, she was on her feet, running from the room. Her movement startled everyone and Brock was on his feet, heading after his daughter, when Dallas rose. A hand on the older man's arm, he shook his head.

"May I? She may speak with me over a family member."

Brock hesitated, a prayer rising for his daughter from his heart before he nodded.

———

"Please? Find out what you can and if she will let you share. She just appeared three days ago, told us that she was moving home, and didn't say why or if it is permanent. She just hasn't talked about it. Devin said she seems haunted."

"Haunted? That could be." Dallas walked rapidly after her, stuffing his feet into his boots and grabbing his jacket. He left the occupants in the room staring after them, all praying for them.

His one hand on Deri's wrist, Dallas simply reached for her phone to prevent her from pitching it across the lawn.

"Deri?" When she didn't respond, he ducked his head to look at her downturned face, seeing the abject horror and fear on it. "Deri? What is it?" When she didn't respond, he reached to wrap her into a hug, feeling the shudders running through her. He looked down at her phone and drew in a deep breath. "You know her?"

Deri nodded, her hair brushing at his jaw. "I do. It's why I came home. Whoever it was had been stalking a group of about twelve of us. We were acquaintances, all involved in the music business in different ways. We are from different countries, which makes it difficult to track. We had gone to the police but they said there wasn't enough evidence to make an investigation. We all thought that we weren't believed. The threats escalated." She drew a shaky breath, sobs choking off her words. "He killed her. He threatened all of us. And we don't know why."

Dallas' arms tightened around her even as he stared at Breck and Barnabas standing behind her, Devin in front of them. He could see Brock and Beck off to the side as well.

"Tell you what. You let me have all the information that you have. I'll look into it. I still have friends on the force who will help. And I know a couple who would be delighted to help." Dallas set her back a bit from him. "Please, Deri? Let me help."

"He'll hurt you. He threatened to do that." She stared up at him, her eyes tear-drenched, endearing her to him even more.

"They always do. We need to talk to your folks. They need to know so that they can watch out."

Deri nodded, not seeing the grim looks on the men's faces before they turned and headed for the house. She jumped as she heard a snap, her eyes finding Dallas', seeing the shock in them as he fell towards her, taking her to the ground, her body trapped under his. She couldn't see the crimson red stain that was widening on his back but she knew that he had been hurt. She lay still, praying for them, seeing the puffs of snow flying up from around them, feeling the sharp shards of some ice crystals as they hit her face before a blow slashed across her temple, driving her down into darkness. Neither heard the yells from the men nor saw Breck take Brock down to the ground, bullets just missing the two of them.

Chapter 2

Breck struggled with his uncle, trying to keep him on the ground. Brock shoved at him, his feet digging into the ground, desperate to reach his daughter. Breck tightened his hold, his head buried against his uncle as puffs of snow kicked up around them. He felt a hand on his arm and raised his head just enough to see that Devin had taken advantage of the breaks in the shots to crawl towards them. He lent his weight to keep his father down.

"Dad! No! We can't move! One of us will die if we do!" Devin's voice finally reached through the terror for his daughter that flooded Brock's mind and he stopped struggling.

"I need to get to her, Devin. Please?" Brock's head was tilted upright, his eyes on the unmoving couple that lay fifteen feet from them.

"We can't, Dad. He's targeting you now." Devin looked around as best he could. "Breck?"

"Yeah?" Breck shot him a glance before he searched the area. "I can't see who it is. It looks as if whoever it might be is around the barn."

"That's what we thought." Devin darted a glance behind him, seeing Barnabas, Bruce, and Beck hunched down on the front veranda, searching as well before their eyes would come back to the couple.

They could hear the rising and falling of the emergency vehicle sirens as they approached before they were cut off. The red and blue emergency lights cut garishly through the deepening twilight. Officers ran towards the men, had them on their feet, and heading for the house, remaining between the men and where the shots had been coming from.

The senior paramedic was on his knees beside Dallas and Deri, a hand to Dallas' back, breathing a sigh of relief that Dallas was still alive. His partner was on the other side and drew in a deep breath.

"It's Dallas."

"What?" His partner looked up before he leaned over. "It is. Guys? Call Will. It's Dallas."

The nearby officers who were standing there to provide protection spun before they looked at one another. One of the officers ducked and ran for his patrol car, the door open to provide protection as he called in to dispatch. Dallas was a fellow officer, a detective, who had just taken his long-overdue vacation

The paramedics worked quickly to stabilize Dallas and Deri before they pushed the stretchers rapidly to the paramedic rigs and then slammed the doors to close them in, heading off with them rapidly, police escort in place.

Brock and Beth stood, arms around one another, Devin beside them as they watched before Bruce pointed to Brock's car.

"Keys, Brock. I'll drive you." Brock fished them out and headed that way, Beth and Elizabeth on their heels.

Breck turned as an officer approached, questions being asked.

"I'm sorry. I don't know why. We had been out here watching them and then headed back in. I think Deri had received a text message. Dallas offered to speak with her."

"Any idea what it was?"

Devin shook his head. "No, she didn't say anything. She has only been home from England for about three days. And before you ask, she didn't say why or if it was permanent. Mom, Dad and I didn't push. You can't with Deri. Not when she was still at home and certainly not now. We knew that she was hiding something but until she said something, we had decided not to push." He stared at the blood-stained snow. "Maybe we should have."

"Wouldn't have made any different, Devin. Not this time." Beck spoke from beside his nephew, an arm around his shoulders. "Is there anything else?"

The officer shook his head. "We'll be here for a while. If you leave me keys to the house, I'll lock up for you, Devin." The officer was a friend of the family. "I know you want to head off."

Devin fished out his keys, dropping them into the outstretched hand. "Thanks, Brad. You know where we'll be." Devin stood, looking around at the scene, worry for his sister and friend uppermost in his mind, but devastation showing on his face. Neasa wrapped an arm around him and turned him, Breck on his other side, Bonnie and Beck following.

"Did they say much about their condition?" Bonnie looked towards the two younger men.

"No, they didn't. Not that they would. Deri had a head wound from the looks of it. Dallas was hit in the back." Breck blinked hard, not willing to let the tears that tickled at his eyes fall. Neasa moved to stand beside him and wrapped her arm around his, her hand finding his.

Brock approached them as they entered the Emergency Department, a sigh rising, knowing that Breck had done this so many times in the last couple of years.

"No word, yet. They're still examining them. They asked if we knew who was Dallas' next of kin."

Breck shrugged. "He has not said but I would suspect his sister or brother. But they're not here. Has anyone called them?"

"Will was." Brock referred to Will Peters, Chief of Police for their town. "I know Dallas is off on leave right now, but he is still a detective with the force. Will started to say something and then stopped."

Breck nodded. "It's not common knowledge." His eyes were on Barnabas who was nodding. "He has shared with us, asking for prayer. I'm not breaking a confidence. At least, I don't think I am. He is on leave right now, taking his accrued vacation. He's looking into leaving the force and taking up a new position. He hasn't said what."

"I have Andy on standby to fly out and bring them in if that's what needed. Doc Whitson is on duty today. He simply looked at me and shook his head." Bruce appeared beside them. "He's spoken to them. They've given permission, his sister faxed it into them, for them to speak with you, Breck, or Barnabas, if a decision has to be made for treatment before they get here."

Chapter 3

Listening as Doc spoke with them, Brock and Beth stood just outside the room Deri lay in. Doc's face was grim but kindly as he spoke to his long-time friends.

"Deri has a wound slashing across her right temple. I spoke with the officers. They feel it was a ricochet that hit her."

"Ricochet?" Brock's arm tightened around Beth. "How is she?"

"Right now? She's starting to rouse but I don't expect that to happen fully yet. Other than that, she is okay. We won't know the extent of her injury until she is fully awake and we can assess her."

"Doc? Any fracture?" Beth's voice held tears.

"No. That is one thing we know for certain. And we can't see any bleeding on the brain, which was a concern. So far, it would be what we term a flesh wound, not that it's any consolation."

"Can we see her?" Beth turned her head, watching her daughter.

"Sure. Go ahead. We'll keep her here for a while. I'm not certain that we will admit her for overnight. We're stretched for beds."

Brock nodded as he followed Beth towards their daughter. An arm around his wife, his finger lightly touched Deri's cheek.

"God was good, Beth. She's not dead or hurt worse."

"No, she's not. Who?"

"Will said his officers were working on it. They need to talk with her. He muttered something about an incident in London."

"Is that why she ran?"

Brock sighed. "I think it was. They handed Devin her phone but it's locked. We don't know what it was that she saw."

"Dallas does, only he can't answer any questions. Any word on him?" Beth was concerned about their young friend. He had endeared himself to them both over the years, but in particular when Breck and Neasa faced the danger from her step-father.

"No, I haven't heard other than they were assessing him. Bruce is making arrangements to bring in his sister and brother."

"Good." Beth's hand rested on her daughter's hair as she prayed for her. "Why did Deri come home?"

"I don't know, sweetheart. She hasn't said. I was planning on having a talk with her in the next couple of days. I still want to but I'm not sure that she will say anything."

"I don't think that she has a choice, not anymore." Beth looked around as she heard footsteps. "Will?"

"Beth. Brock. I'm here as your friend. Nothing more right now. The officers are investigating. They will update as they can but I have asked that I not be involved in the investigation. We're too close of friends." He stood watching them before he turned his attention to Deri. "How is she?"

"Flesh wound is what Doc called it." Brock's hand clenched into a fist. "Who did this, Will?"

"We have no idea. We'll need to speak with Deri when she's able to." Will hesitated. "I'll be in the waiting room. Daniel was around and has the church prayer chain working."

"Thank him for us." Brock hesitated. "I'll leave and send in Devin, love."

Beth nodded. "He needs to see her." She accepted her husband's hug and watched them leave, to find Devin beside her in no time, worry on his face for his younger sister.

"Mom?"

"Just the wound. Nothing more serious yet that they know of. Have you any word on Dallas?"

"No, not really. Other than they were thinking surgery. I was with Breck and Barnabas when the surgeon came out. They're with him now."

"Oh, I see. We'll pray for him."

"We will, Mom. Some of the Foundation building family are here. They wanted you to know that they are meeting in the chapel, holding a prayer vigil for these two." Devin's arm was around his mother as she wept for a moment before she controlled herself.

"Thank them for me." She looked around as a nurse approached, an apology on her face. "That's okay, nurse. Just come get us when we can come back in."

Chapter 4

Standing in Dallas' room with the surgeon, Breck and Barnabas listened carefully, their eyes on first the surgeon and then their friend. Dallas was on his stomach, and they could see the dressings taped to his back, pressure on the wounds to help stop the bleeding if possible.

"You're talking surgery?" Breck asked, his attention on the surgeon.

"We are. He was hit in the shoulder blade area on the right side and the bullet deflected up towards his shoulder. He may have been moving at the time that he was hit. We can feel the bullet, so it's not that difficult of surgery. Just a matter of cleaning the wounds, ensuring there is no damage from the bullet's trajectory. Not an overlong surgery."

"Can you do it here or do you need to take him to the operating room?" Barnabas was thinking of all the scenarios that he could.

"We can do it here. We're pushing for operating time today. If we wait for that, it may be tomorrow." He looked between the two men. "It's your decision, I am told. I hear that his sister and his brother are on their way, but we should do this now."

Breck nodded, reaching for the clipboard, and scrawled his name. "When?"

"Give us about thirty minutes. You can stay with him until then." The surgeon made a final assessment and then walked away, fatigue starting to hit him. He had been on call for a couple of days now and it had been busy.

Three hours later, Breck stood once more beside Dallas' bed, watching his friend as he moved restlessly. He was starting to rouse, the effects of the shock and then the anesthesia wearing off. Breck had been told that Dallas' family were heading in. They had chosen to drive, rather than have Andy come for them, but it would be a couple of hours yet before they got there. He turned as he heard footsteps. Brock approached.

"How is he, Breck?" Brock stopped by the bedside, his eyes on his young friend.

"Waking up. He was fortunate, the surgeon said. A lot less damage than they expected. All soft tissue, which will heal. He may need some physiotherapy but they aren't even sure about that. Not until he's up and moving the arm."

"Thank God He was there, protecting the two of them. I don't know what the outcome would have been." Brock had been puzzled all the afternoon, his thoughts discussed with Bruce and Beck, with Will chiming in. "Do we know if it was Deri or Dallas that was the target?"

"That we don't know. We've been trying to figure that one out." Breck looked at his uncle. "Deri? How is she?"

"On her feet and angry. And I don't blame her. She has a bad headache, she says, which is to be expected." Brock laid a hand on Dallas' shoulder, praying for him. "She wants to see him."

"I guess that's okay. Just let her know that he's not awake." Breck turned to look behind him and then reached out a hand for Deri. "Deri? Should you be walking?"

"I'm not travelling in that four-wheel contraption called a wheelchair." Deri's voice was disgruntled, and Breck could hear the anger in it. She stopped as she saw Dallas before her hand was out to touch his cheek. "Breck?"

"He's waking up, Deri. It will be a bit." Breck shared a look with Brock. "You need to go home and sleep."

"I can't. Not until I talk to him." Deri looked up, a look on her face that Breck and Brock had never seen before. "I need to know if it was because of me."

"We don't know that, Deri." Brock fished out her phone and handed it to her. "The police have asked what it was that you had been looking at before you ran from the house."

Deri shook in fear for a moment before she took her phone. "It's brutal, Dad. I know you have wanted to talk to me, about why I came home. I was trying to stay under the radar, not letting anyone know where I was or why. I guess that didn't work as well." She looked around. "There was a detective here earlier. Davy?"

———

"That's right. Davy. He's still here, hoping to speak with you." Brock swung an arm around his daughter, turning her from the bed and walking towards the door. "Breck will come and get you once you can see Dallas."

Chapter 5

The detective that had been waiting, Detective Davy Smithson, looked up as he heard footsteps and rose. Brock nodded at him before he helped Deri to a seat.

"Deri, this is Detective Smithson. He's been wanting to speak with you."

Deri studied him, looked down at her phone before she unlocked it and found the picture still there. She thrust her phone at him.

"Here. This is what I saw. Dallas is the only one other than myself who has seen it."

Davy studied her and then looked down at the picture and grimaced. "This is brutal, Deri. You know her?"

"I do. There were about twelve of us that hung around together in London. We were all involved in music. I had recorded a digital album and they were on some of the songs. We started getting vague threats and just shrugged them off. When we started getting packages of photos of us that had us crossed off, we went to the police. It was shrugged off as just an annoying fan. We kept getting them, each one worse than the one before. We would ask for help, an investigation, and were basically told that the police would not get involved. That we were likely sending them to ourselves to stir up publicity. We never went to the papers with these. We were too scared to."

"I see." Davy sent the photo on to his own phone and then looked up at her. "Do you have any more of these?"

"I have them saved to a file on my laptop. I can get them to you." Deri's hands rubbed up and down her arms, remembered fear clouding her thoughts.

"That would be good. How be I stop by tomorrow and retrieve them to a thumb drive?" At her nod, he looked thoughtful. "Who knew that you were moving home?"

"Just that girl and one another. I shut my flat, handed the keys to the landlord, and came home. I didn't have a lot to bring. Most of what I had? I didn't want to keep it. I felt it was tainted by what I was going through."

"I can understand that." He shared a look with Brock. "Now, about what happened earlier today. What can you remember?"

Deri's brow wrinkled. "Not a lot. I saw that picture and ran from the house. Dallas came after me, said he had told Dad that he would talk with me. He asked what was wrong. Dallas had taken the phone as he hugged me. I could feel him tense as he looked down. We only had a chance to talk just a bit when I heard a snap, saw the look of horror on his face, and then he fell towards me, taking me down with him. I didn't move, not sure what was going on. Then I don't remember much."

—

"That's okay. You were unconscious. So it's natural that you won't." Davy looked down at his notes, fear for the young lady in front of him in his mind. "What else can you tell me about these other eleven ladies?"

Deri stared at him and then described what she knew about them, their lives, their names, birthdates, what they did in the music business. "I'm not much help." She finally conceded that she really didn't know a lot about them. "We usually talked about work and where we wanted to be, rather than personal stuff."

"That okay. You've given me enough that I can get started on the investigation. I'll be in touch if I have more questions, and I am sure that I will. Here's my card. Call me if you think of anything more." Davy walked away, leaving Deri staring down at the little piece of cardboard before Brock reached for it and tucked it into a pocket.

Deri looked up as she felt her father's arm around her and heard him begin to pray. Her head went down on his shoulder.

"I'm sorry, Dad." Her voice was quiet as she spoke, his prayer finished. "I should have told you but I was so scared. I didn't want to worry you."

"We were anyway, love. You know that you can talk to us about anything."

"I know. It's just that I've been on my own for so many years that it's difficult to do that."

"We understand that, Deri. We won't intrude but please? Talk to us?" Brock watched his daughter carefully and drew a deep breath. She's not going to, is she, Lord?

"If I can, Dad. But if it puts you in danger, I can't."

"But if it puts us into danger, that's exactly when you need to."

Deri sat for a moment before she gave an abrupt nod and was on her feet, moving carefully so that the headache didn't worsen as she walked towards Dallas' room, hoping and praying that he might be awake by then. Brock stood and watched her before he followed her, eyes sorrowful at what he had heard. Lord, she's hurting, not just physically. I can't imagine what she has been through. Thank you for bringing her home, dear Lord, but we need to solve this and help her heal. I sense that she is struggling with her faith. Help her to return to You.

Chapter 6

Reaching out an arm to hug his cousin, Breck watched her for a moment and then nodded. She seemed a bit different, he thought, but like her father, he sensed her struggles.

"Talk to Davy?"

"I did. He has asked hard questions." She leaned her head against his arm. "Why did I ever think I could do that, move across the ocean and make a life for myself?"

"You always wanted to live in London. And your music is reaching people. I know that." Breck studied her again. "What can we do, Neasa and I, to help you?"

She shrugged. "I'm not sure anyone can do anything. What I was going through in London was shoved to the side by the authorities. They actually told us that we were sending the photos and that stuff to ourselves." She didn't see Breck's grim look or the look on her brother's face as he stood behind her. "We weren't. And now one of the twelve of us is dead. Murdered. But they'll likely say one of us did it or that she killed herself."

"I doubt that is the case, sis." Devin moved to stand beside her, watching as Dallas had roused and was, in turn, watching Deri.

"It is, Devin. It's what the authorities said. They said it was a publicity stunt that we came up with. Davy

—

30

believed me, I think, but I don't know what he can do from here."

"He'll talk to them. We also have a friend and his wife who will get involved, if we ask. They will work on it."

Deri shook her head, turning to find Dallas watching her. "Dallas? You're awake. How are you?"

"Hurting. Hurting for you, Deri. I wish I could go over there and set them straight."

"It wouldn't work. It never does, does it?" Deri watched as he digested her words and then nodded.

"We'll work on it. I'm on leave from the force but I still have access to what I need."

Deri shook her head. "No, don't. Leave it for someone else. They will say that you are looking for revenge if you do."

"She has a point, Dallas." Devin swung an arm around his sister. "Sis, you need to come with me. Say good night to Dallas. I'll bring you back in the morning. How long are you here for?"

"Until tomorrow." Breck spoke up. "We'll make sure that these two see each other."

Dallas watched as she walked away before he drew a deep breath, grimacing with pain as he did so. What had he gone and done? He looked up at Breck, finding Breck staring at the floor, a look of frustration on his face.

"Breck?" Dallas waited until Breck looked at him. "What happened? And don't spare any details.

—

I've been shot before. I am thinking that is what happened."

"You were. In the back. The surgeon said the bullet hit the shoulder blade and deflected upwards to your shoulder. He seems to think that you were moving forward when it happened and that changed the angle that you were hit."

"I was, I think. I can remember looking at Deri's phone and then moving to hug her. She's so tiny that I had to bend over to do that." He looked thoughtful. "Is that why?"

"More than likely. Listen. Your sister and your brother are on their way in."

Dallas groaned. "Not that, please. I moved here to get away from Susan. She wants to run my life even though she is three years younger than me. I can't handle that right now. Sean is okay. He's about a year younger than me and understood totally. Susan got worse after our parents and our youngest sister, Sandra, were killed in a home invasion."

"I'm sorry, Dallas. I don't think that we ever knew that." Breck pulled up a chair and sat. "You never talked about your home life, other than to mention your sister and brother."

"It still hurts, Breck. Even after all these years." Dallas blinked to clear away the tears. "We were close. Dad was a pastor, Mom a teacher. Sandra was only in Grade eight when it happened. I was just finishing high school. Because I was eighteen, I could take on the care of Susan and Sean. Susan has been angry for years about that. I finished my degree and then moved here.

By that time, she was eighteen and could be on her own. I just couldn't do it, not at that time. She has continued in the same way, wanting to control my life."

"That's never good." Breck studied his friend, praying for him. "How do I pray for you, Dallas?"

"For peace, I guess. I'm pretty beaten up right now. Beaten up and burnt out." He held up a hand as Breck opened his mouth. "No, it's not what you all went through. There were other cases, cases that we can't resolve that haunt me. That and I am really struggling right now to see God in everything."

"Now I know how to pray for you. May I share with Neasa?"

"Of course." Dallas looked up at the commotion at the door and groaned. "You may want to duck out, Breck. Susan is here."

"I'll stay for a bit and then head out. Deri will want to see you again tomorrow. Let me know when you're checking out."

"I will. Thanks, my friend." Dallas held up a hand as Susan sent to hug him. "Not now, Susan. You can't."

"And just why can't I?" She still reached before Sean caught her arm. "What?" She turned on him.

"Susan, we discussed it. He has a wound to his back. He can't be moving around a lot tonight, not after surgery. And it will hurt him a lot if you try."

—

"Oh! Well, then, I guess I won't." She turned to stare at Breck, who simply stared back at her, an amused look in his eyes that had her glaring at him in his turn.

Chapter 7

Standing in the hallway outside Dallas' room the next morning, Deri hesitated about entering. It was just before visiting hours started and she had made Devin bring her, although he had offered to before she had finished her request. She entered slowly, looking around, before her eyes found Dallas, finding him seated in a chair in the room, fully dressed.

"Hi." She walked towards him, taking the hand that he reached out to her. "How are you?"

"Sore, as you can imagine. Grateful. Thankful." He looked up at her, taking in once more her beauty, even with the whiteness of her face and the dark shadows under her eyes. "And you?"

Deri shrugged. "Okay, I guess. I didn't sleep a lot. It was hard to get comfortable."

"I'm sure that it was. Listen. We need to talk. Not just about what happened." Dallas studied her, seeing the faint blush on her face. "Nothing pressing, but I would like to talk with you about what happened in London. If you will."

"Sure." She lifted a shoulder. "I don't think that it will make any difference, though. Davy was around earlier this morning, picking my brain as he called it. I gave him a copy of all the photos."

"And I am sure that you have many." Dallas looked towards the door and groaned. "I was hoping to spare you Susan this morning. Guess that didn't work."

Deri gave him a puzzled look and then turned to the door, facing his sister and brother, not realizing that they were still holding hands.

Susan took a look and her and the look turned into a glare. "Who is she? And why is she here? She can leave anytime. I'm here."

Sean drew in his breath, ready to tell Susan that this was the young lady who had been hurt when Dallas had been when Dallas spoke up.

"That's enough, Susan. This is a friend." His hand tightened on Deri's as she pulled at his grasp to release her hand. "Don't speak to her that way."

"I'm your sister. I will if I want to. You can leave. You're not needed here." Her tone plainly said that Deri wasn't wanted either.

Deri pulled her hand free, her face whiter than it had been, and blinked at the tears that she could not stop from falling. Dallas had pushed himself to his feet, anger on his face as he stared at his sister before he reached for Deri, finding her gone. He stared at the door and then at Sean.

"She's gone, Dallas. I couldn't stop her." He had walked to the door, searching for her and finding her disappearing into the elevator, a man around her age with her.

"No, I didn't think that you would." He turned on Susan. "Susan, get out of my sight. Right now, I am so angry with you that I'm forgetting you are my sister. And that I am a Christian. Leave." He turned to the cupboard, reaching for a jacket that Scan had brought him. "Sean, find me transportation. I'm leaving."

"You can't. You're not discharged. Besides, you're not well enough to be going anywhere." Susan still protested, even as Sean glared at her.

"Just shut up, Susan. Enough already!" Sean turned to speak with Dallas, to find him gone. "Now? See what you've done? Dallas isn't well enough to be out there. Not on his own. And you have driven him to that."

"I did no such thing. She did!" Susan jumped as Sean grabbed her arm and dragged her from the room and down the stairs, finding Breck at the bottom. "Breck? Where's the bus station? Susan is heading there."

"I am doing no such thing!" Susan tried to drag her arm from her brother's grasp, finding it impossible to do that. "Let me go!"

"Not until I put you on a bus for home. You've done enough damage this time, Susan. We'll be lucky if Dallas even speaks with us again. Are you satisfied?"

Breck stood uncomfortable for a moment. "I can take her there if you like."

"Where is your vehicle? Yes, if you don't mind. She needs to go. She just insulted Deri." Sean watched as Breck's face turned grim.

"You insulted Deri? And she's injured as well."

"That's too bad. It's her fault, isn't it, that Dallas was hurt?" Susan stood her ground, unwilling to back down

"No. Actually, we don't know that for a fact. It could have been Dallas that the sniper was after." Breck stood by his truck door, opening it and motioning. "In you go."

Susan refused. Sean stared at her and then at the patrol officer who had appeared.

"Problem, Breck?"

"Sam? Yes. This young lady needs to go to the bus station and be put on a bus home. She insulted Deri."

"She did, did she?" Sam turned his attention to Susan, watching Sean at the same time. "Insulted our Deri, did you? That doesn't happen. Sorry. You're his brother?"

"I am. Sean Chisholm. This is our sister, Susan."

"All righty, then. Susan, if you will come with me?"

"No, I won't."

"Sorry, Miss. I'm asking in an official manner. If you don't come, then I have to arrest you for refusing a police command."

Susan finally flounced to the patrol car and stood at the back door that was ajar, opened her mouth to speak, and thought better of it, seating herself, not looking around at anyone, Sam shook his head, spoke to the two men, and then headed away.

<hr>

"Sean? Did Dallas leave anything in his room?"

Sean thought for a moment. "Just some flowers, I think. We need to get them."

"We can. Then I'll take you to my uncle's. That is more than likely where he is." Breck stood for a moment, staring the way the patrol car had gone, a prayer raised for Susan. She was a soul who needed that, no matter how angry she was.

Chapter 8

Brock looked up as the door to the kitchen opened and Deri appeared. He frowned as he glanced over at the clock. She shouldn't be home yet. It had not been all that long since Devin had driven off with her. Deri didn't speak, simply kicked off her shoes, hung up her jacket and disappeared. Brock listened, hearing the faint plunking of discordant notes front the piano. He sighed. Something had gone very wrong, he thought.

Devin stood for a moment, his coat hung up on the rack before he reached for the coffee pot and poured himself one, sitting at the table with his father. He idly reached for the hymnal that his father had open.

"Picking out the songs for Sunday, Dad?"

"I am. Daniel wants one that goes with hope." He looked at his son. "What happened?"

Devin shrugged. "I'm not sure, Dad." He looked towards the hallway. "Deri was in with Dallas, I had made sure of that. I was in the waiting room when I think it was his sister and brother who appeared. They disappeared into the room. I could hear a louder voice and then Deri appeared. She was crying, Dad, silent tears that broke my heart. I don't know what happened and she won't talk about it. She just refused to say a word. Just asked me to bring her home."

"I see." Brock sighed. "One of us will need to talk to her. Let her have some time to compose herself. Mom's to be home shortly. Maybe she'll talk to her."

"I wouldn't count on that, Dad. Now, your hymns? Just hymns or worship choruses?"

"Both, I think." The men were soon lost in their discussion, the notes from the piano turning from despair to a tune, not one that they recognized.

Devin finally disappeared, a glance at the clock telling him that he was needed at work. He hesitated to leave and finally stopped in the family room doorway to watch his sister, praying for her.

Looking up some time later, Brock rose and headed for the door, stepping back to let Dallas enter. He frowned as he saw the whiteness of the younger man's face, the pain on it, but the determination showing in his eyes.

"Brock? I'm sorry. I'm looking for Deri. Is she here?"

Brock nodded, a stern look on his own face. "She is, Dallas. Come in."

"Can I see her?" Dallas didn't take his eyes away from the older man.

"You may be able to. She's been hurt, Dallas. What happened?"

Dallas sighed. "My sister. She told Deri to leave, that she was not needed there. She spoke out of turn."

"I see. My little girl was hurt deeply by this, young man. I will let you go through to see her but

—

understand this. This never happens again." Brock watched with compassion as Dallas' eyes slid closed and then he nodded.

"I understand, Brock. I wasn't able to stop Susan and Deri was gone before we could stop her. Sean went after her but she was already on the elevator."

"I know. She told me." Brock's hand was on Dallas' good shoulder. "Let me pray for you first, Dallas. You're hurting and only the Good Lord has the ability to comfort and heal you." He was as good as his word.

Dallas hesitated when he was finished before he moved towards the hallway, following the sound of music. He tilted his head. No, he decided, he didn't know that tune. He listened as Deri went back and forth with notes, finally seeming to be satisfied. Watching from the doorway, Dallas wasn't sure if he should enter or not, and that was unlike him. But then again, he decided, he had never been in such a situation. The young lady that he was beginning to care about, even on such short acquaintance was hurting, hurt by his own sister, and he didn't know how to approach her.

Making his feet move forward at long last, Dallas stood beside Deri, just watching as she jotted notes down on a paper music sheet, nodding to herself as she did so. I have no idea what she's doing but I don't care. She's here and so am I.

"Deri?"

Deri froze as she heard his voice before she continued what she was doing.

"I'm sorry. I didn't know that Susan would do that." He perched on the edge of the piano seat before she shifted over to let him sit. "Can we talk?"

Brock stood watching the two, their shoulders touching before he shook his head. Lord, they need help, don't they?

When Dallas had walked away from his sister, he had had no idea of where he was going, only that he wanted to find Deri and do that quickly. Stopping at the nurses' station, he had simply said that he was leaving, taking the discharge papers handed to him and tucking them into an inside pocket of his jacket. Ignoring the question of how he was getting home, he had headed for the elevator, impatient to leave.

A hand on his arm in the sling, he had tucked his head down into his jacket, the collar pulled up and a woollen hat on his head. It was warmer, he thought, and the snow that he had fallen into the day before was rapidly melting.

He had overestimated his strength, Dallas finally admitted, fatigue weighing his feet down. He refused to stop. Refused to ask for help. All he knew was that every step took him one more step towards Deri. That Susan had deeply hurt her, he knew. Susan's animosity to everyone had finally done it, he thought. She has driven a rift into the family, and right now, Lord, I don't know that we can repair it. It's in Your hands. I don't even know what Sean will do. And that is not where my concern is right now.

Davy passed him, slowing his vehicle as he frowned, before he turned, drove by him and then turned to come to a stop near him. He was out of the vehicle and standing in front of Dallas, a hand out to balance him as he stopped.

"Dallas? Have you been discharged? I was on my way to find you." Davy was concerned, the whiteness and tenseness of the other man's face showing how much he was hurting.

"Davy? Can you help me find Deri?" There was desperation in his plea.

"Deri? Isn't she at home?" Davy steered Dallas to his vehicle, tucking him inside before he ran around to the driver's side and slid behind the wheel.

"She had come to see me." Dallas sighed, his eyes closing at the memory. "Susan took offence at her being there and insulted her. Deri left before we could stop her. I don't know where she went." He looked over at Davy. "Can you find her for me?"

"I can try. Do you know who she was with?"

Dallas shrugged. "I don't know. Sean said a young man, but I don't know who."

"Her brother, likely. Let's head that way. First, you need a coffee. And so do I." Davy pulled into a popular diner and was in and out in short order with their coffees. He handed one to Dallas. "Now, what else can you tell me?"

"Not much." Dallas was silent, watching the streets of the town that he called home, that he loved, and that he was no longer sure would be home to him. He was searching, for what he wasn't quite sure.

—

Dallas had thanked Davy for the ride and then stood, his eyes on the lawn, seeing the disturbed snow and knowing that one of his fellow officers had taken steps to remove the blood. He was thankful for that. He turned to stare at the house, his emotions in a roil, not sure if he should be there or not.

He had tapped at the kitchen door, finding Brock just standing and watching him as he entered, not saying anything. He had been prayed for and then sent to find Deri.

Deri had not looked around as she heard the whisper of socked feet on the hardwood floor, thinking that it was one of her family. Only it wasn't. She had simply moved over so that Dallas could sit beside her, their shoulders touching, as she continued to pick out the tune that she was writing. Her hands were finally still.

Dallas had not said much since sitting down. He had simply watched as she worked, knowing that he could not and would not disturb her.

"Deri? I am so sorry for what Susan said to you. She was out of line."

"Was she? Really?" He could hear the slight scorn in her voice.

"She was. She does not decide who I see or don't see. That's part of the reason that I moved here."

"Is it? And how's that going?" Deri sighed. "It's my turn to apologize. I just don't seem to be able to do anything right today." She flipped at the music sheets. "Even this is not working."

"It's not?" Dallas stared down at his index finger before he starting to pick out the tune she had been playing.

Deri's head tilted as she listened, hearing what she had done played by someone else. Her hand stopped his. "Dallas? You just solved something for me." Deri was lost in her music, leaving Dallas to watch her and follow as best he could.

Brock and Beth watched from the doorway before they turned, arms around one another.

"He's here, isn't he?" Beth was confused. "I thought that he would be with his family."

"There's a problem there. From what he told me, his sister insulted Deri and Deri fled before he could stop her. I would imagine that his sister is on her way home. I have no idea where his brother is. I think that he said Sean was still in town."

"He sent his own sister away over Deri? Oh, that will go over well, I would imagine." Beth began to rummage in the fridge for the makings of a meal. When Brock didn't respond, she looked over the fridge door. "Brock?"

"Hmm?" Brock shook his head, smiling at Beth. "Sorry. I was lost in thought. What was that you said?"

"That Dallas chose Deri over his sister and how well that would go over."

"I'm not worried about it. Dallas said his sister is angry and that he moved here to get away from her. At least, I think that is what he said."

"Men! Can't remember anything." Beth smirked at her husband. "How long do you think they'll talk?"

"If they're like us, they'll talk until they clear the air or someone grows frustrated and walks away. We do that, hon, but we always talk it through."

"That we do." Beth agreed even as she prayed for her daughter and the young man with her.

Chapter 10

Deri finally set the music aside, satisfied that she had found the tune she needed for the lyrics that had been sent to her. She needed to refine it but the basics were there. She eyed Dallas as he sat beside her, lost in thought, his eyes on the keyboard.

"Dallas? How did you get here?" Her question brought his eyes to her.

"I started walking." Dallas had looked away and then back at her as she gave a shocked noise.

"You starting walking? Do you know how far it is?"

Dallas shrugged. "Far. But Davy came by and dropped me off. We need to talk, Deri, and I mean really talk. I am sorry about Susan. She has had that attitude since before Mom and Dad were killed."

"I'm sorry about your parents. And it was a sister?" At his nod, she wrapped an arm around his, her head resting against his shoulder. "How is your shoulder? And don't tell me fine."

"It hurts and I know it will hurt more as it starts to heal." Dallas sat for a moment, content just to be beside her. "How is your head?"

"It hurts. I shouldn't be doing this." She flipped a finger at the music sheets. "But I promised the tune by the end of this week and it's getting close to that. I

—

need to refine it, but thanks to you, I have it almost written." She smiled up at him. "You'll get credit on it."

"Oh, no. I don't need that."

"But you do." She was silent for a while before she spoke again. "I was so scared, Dallas, when I saw the look in your eyes. I thought you were dead."

"You did? I don't really remember much other than the blow and seeing you fading in my vision. Davy said that they haven't found who it was. There wasn't a lot of evidence. They're not even sure which one of us it was meant for."

'They're not? I thought it was me." Deri had to think about that. "But why you?"

"I'm a police officer, Deri. You know that. I have had threats against me over my career." He paused, a sad look flickering across his face. "I decided to do that when my parents and sister were murdered. It's not what I wanted to do, but it's who I have become. Until now."

"Until now? Please, explain." Deri studied his face, seeing a finality cross it.

"I'm on leave right now, taking my accrued vacation. When that ends, my resignation takes effect. I will be taking on a new role at the Barnabas Foundation, that of investigations. We're still working through what, but it will be free to those who cannot afford to pay. But there are parameters that are being set up."

"You will be good at that. I can tell. I heard how you have helped your friends there." Deri turned as she heard a sound and found Devin walking towards us. "Devin?"

"Sis. Dallas. Mom has supper ready. She said to warn you it will be on the table in five minutes and if you wanted any, you needed to wash up."

"Will do, brother of mine. Dallas, you're invited for supper." Deri was on her feet, walking rapidly away. The men could hear her voice in the kitchen talking to her mother.

"What happened today, Dallas? Deri was in tears and she does not cry, not in public." Devin was throwing the big brother act and both men knew it.

"My sister. Told her to leave, that she wasn't needed. Only the implication was that she wasn't wanted. She didn't speak for me. As far as I know, she is on her way home."

"She is? Are you sure about that? I won't have my sister hurt again." Devin was stern.

"Nor should she be. Susan was made aware that she doesn't talk to my friends like that. Sean tried to stop her as well." Dallas sighed. "I have no idea where he is at present."

Devin looked around as he heard Breck behind him.

"Breck?"

"Your sister was escorted to the bus station and put on a bus to her home. She was strictly lectured by the officer who took her there. Your brother is hurting for you, Dallas. He's not sure if you will want to see him. Sean said to tell you that he'll stay at your place for tonight and then head for home. He has some meetings that he couldn't reschedule."

"No, he can't. Thanks, Breck. How much trouble did she give you?" He gave a grim smile as Breck just shrugged. "You just said what you didn't say. I know her. Thanks for letting me know about Sean." He stood and then staggered, the pain hitting in a rush. He didn't hear the exclamation from Breck before he moved in to catch him as he collapsed.

With Devin's help, they moved him to the couch in the room, Devin calling for his mother. Deri was here before he had finished, on her knees beside the couch, a hand on Dallas' face.

"What happened?" Deri looked up as the men didn't answer, finding her mother beside her, her father beside Breck.

"He stood up and then just went down." Devin was worried, his phone out as he moved away. "Sean? It's Devin. Dallas just collapsed. What's that? No, I don't think we'll need to take him there. Here's our address and this is how you get here. Thanks. See you in a bit."

Deri was on her feet, beside her brother. "Devin? Who did you call?"

"Sean. He needs to be here, Deri. You know that."

"I know." She turned as she heard Dallas speaking. "What happened?"

"You just repeated yourself, you know." Devin grinned at her before he sobered. "I would say the pain hit. How long had you two been sitting there?"

Deri paled. "I don't know. A couple of hours I guess. You know me when I get involved in a tune."

"I know, sis. And your head is pounding, isn't it?" Devin wrapped an arm around her, following Breck to the kitchen. "Mom has soup and sandwiches ready. Let's dish up and take it in there. It's not the first time we've eaten in there. Dad was lighting the fire in the fireplace, he said."

Deri nodded, her mind more on Dallas than what her hands were doing. Breck watched her closely, sending her agitation, but also see a certain look on her face that they had waited for years to see. He's the one, is he, Lord? He's a good man. Struggling, but then we all do. Deri will be good for him, won't she, Lord? And he will be so good for her. She needs someone like him.

Chapter 11

Dallas sat up, wiping at the sweat on his brow. The pain had hit in such a hard, abrupt manner that he had been unable to prepare for it. He looked up with thanks as Brock handed him a glass of water and some pain medication and swallowed the tablets quickly. Why, Lord? Who did this? And how do I protect Deri, the lady of my dreams, if I collapse simply from pain? Lord? Are we back on speaking terms? I know that I've really struggled lately but I have felt You with me.

Deri was on the couch beside him, a hand on his arm, concern and fear in her eyes.

"Dallas?"

"It's okay, Deri. Just the pain got me for a moment." He grinned at her. "I guess I shouldn't have been sitting on that bench without a back."

"No, you shouldn't have." She gave him a disgruntled look. She went to say something else but bit back the words.

"You can say it. I was stupid. But I was enjoying watching you work." He continued to grin at her even as he looked up and took the plate of food offered him. "This smells good, Beth."

"Just a simple meal." Beth sat where she could watch them, the flames from the fire reflecting in her glasses. "Brock?"

"Before we eat, let's pray. We have a lot to be thankful for, but we have a lot to request. Our food won't cool off that much during a quick prayer." He was as good as his word.

Devin rose as he heard a tap at the door and admitted Sean.

"Devin?"

"He's up again. It was the pain." Devin gave a low laugh. "Deri was working on a tune and he was seated beside her. Knowing her it was likely a couple of hours."

"A tune?" He took the tray with the bowl of soup and sandwich handed him even as Devin poured the cup of tea that he requested.

"Deri is an artist, a songstress as they used to say. She has an album coming up, her fourth I think. But she writes tunes for lyricists. If she gets involved in that, you don't get her away from the piano until she has the basics down. I suspect that is what happened."

"Deri? I'm not sure that I have heard her works." Sean followed Devin.

"I'll give you the website address for her work. She's good, even if she is my sister."

Dallas looked up as Sean appeared and hugged his brother as he leaned over before he took a seat near him. Devin had claimed his seat beside his sister. The talk was laughter-filled before the men gathered the dishes, stacked them into the dishwasher and then returned to the family room with the tray of sweets and cookies Beth had left ready, the coffee pot and teapot on another tray.

Dallas looked over at Sean, seeing the stress in his brother.

"Sean?"

Sean looked up, an apologetic smile on his face. "I'm sorry, Dallas. I had no idea Susan would do what she did."

"None of us did, I don't think. That doesn't excuse it, though." Dallas looked down at Deri, who sat staring at the flames, a dreamy look on her face. He looked up at Devin, who just smiled and shrugged

Talk turned to the shooting and speculation as to who was responsible. Dallas felt Deri begin to tense as they talked and his hand found hers, squeezing it gently.

"We can stop this talk, if you like, Deri." He leaned over to whisper to her.

She shook her head. "No, we need to talk about it. It just scares me that whoever it is may go after my parents or Devin."

Dallas squeezed her hand again before he reached for his mug of coffee, a thoughtful look on his face.

"We'll figure it out, Deri. That I promise you."

"But who gets hurt in the process and the meanwhile?" Deri's eyes slid closed as she fought the tears that blinded her.

Chapter 12

Dallas looked around, two days later, as he walked through the downtown area. Davy was running towards him.

"Dallas? You're up and about. How are you?" Davy studied the younger man.

Dallas shrugged. "I'm not sure. The pain is there and it's starting to itch." He looked around, finally pointing towards a nearby coffee shop. "Do you have time for coffee?"

"I do. I was actually heading your way in a bit. This works." Davy held the door to the shop, walking in behind Dallas. "Have a seat. Your usual?"

"Sure." Dallas slid into one of the few booths, loosening his jacket and shrugging out of it. It was awkward, he decided, trying to manoeuvre one-handed.

"What news do you have, Davy?" Dallas watched his fellow detective closely.

"Not enough that we can even begin to start more of an investigation. We have not set it aside, Dallas. You know how we work. Will wants me on this. I've even gone to my sources on the streets. Nothing there."

"So is it Deri or me?" Dallas was frustrated. "She's been through so much, on her own. She is hiding, Davy. And I know from what Devin has said that's not her. She's a people person."

"She is. I can tell that by speaking with her." He sipped at his coffee before he returned the mug to the table. "Go over your cases with me, ones where you were threatened. You have those. We all do."

"I do. I guess we can do that here." Dallas began to speak quietly, giving case numbers and what the threat was. "But I don't remember anyone threatening to shoot me. There were all sorts of other threats."

"Okay. I'll speak with these people. Anyone who didn't threaten you that stands out?"

Dallas shrugged. "Not offhand. I can think about it, but I'm not sure that I can come up with anyone." He paused and then shook his head. "No. I can't think of anyone offhand." He paused again, his eyes on Davy. "I know you not likely can say. Anything with London?"

Davy nodded. "There is. I'm heading out to see Deri. Are you on foot?"

"I am. I can't drive yet. I was wandering around down here, bored."

Davy laughed. "I can see that. Come on then, friend. Let's get you to your lady so that I can speak with her." He didn't see the shocked look on Dallas' face and then the softening and smile as he nodded.

She is my lady, isn't she, Lord? But I feel that I am broken and need to recover and return to You. I know that You never moved. I did. I got burnt out and turned away from You instead of to You. Please, dear Lord? Bring me home. Help me to return to You.

Deri stared at the two men standing at the door before she stood back and let them in.

"Can you give me ten minutes or so? I'm on a call that I have to finish."

"Sure." Dallas moved towards the coffee pot. "I'll make us some coffee and for you, the tea that you prefer."

"Thanks, Dallas." She was gone almost before she had finished her words and the men could hear the tinkle of piano keys and her voice as she finished off her call.

Deri hesitated as she replaced her phone on the piano, her thoughts on the music that she was composing. She finally shook her head, turning to face the doorway to the hall. Dallas was in the kitchen, and that made her happy. But Davy was here as well, and that frightened her. He must have news of some kind if he was there. She finally rose, her thoughts still on the tune that she was working on. The lyricist, Elizabeth, had said that Deri had been recommended for her. She had emailed her the lyrics and then had called to follow up. Deri was excited about working with someone so well known but it also scared her.

Dallas rose as Deri finally appeared, a hand out for her, drawing out her chair. He set the cup of tea in front of her before he sat back down, his eyes on her. Her eyes were on Davy, who was watching her closely, a shuttered look on his face.

"You worked the streets." Deri's words were a statement, not a question.

"I did, though I'm not sure how you knew."

"Street cops and those who worked undercover have something about them that says that. I just know who they are. I have always been able to do that."

Davy nodded. "You're good. And that's not for public knowledge, young lady."

"I never say anything. I wouldn't. It would put people at risk." She sipped at her tea before she spoke again. "What news do you have?"

Davy grinned at her. "Direct and to the point. I like that, young lady. Let's see. First, how are you feeling?"

"I still have a headache. That's normal, isn't it?" She shrugged off his concern.

"It is." Davy opened and then closed the folder he had placed on the table beside him. "I would like you to take a look at these photos. Go through them first without saying anything. Once you have gone through them, we talk."

Deri nodded. These photos are going to change things, aren't they, Lord? How do I do this? It's frightening. I'm so scared. She opened the folder, her eyes on Dallas before she looked down. She turned over photo after photo, her face growing whiter with each one. She flipped the pile back over before she looked up at Davy, seeing his compassionate glance.

"You knew!"

"I had a good idea when I saw that photo on your phone. And then the others? That confirmed it." He shared a look with Dallas. "What can you tell me?"

"These are the ladies that I was friends with. Wait!" Deri went back through them. "No, they look like them but they're not. What is going on, Davy?" She looked up at him, her face even whiter than it had been. The two men could feel the fear that enveloped her.

Chapter 13

Dallas reached for her hand, his grasp welcoming to her, as he stared at first Deri and then Davy.

"Deri? You're sure that these are not them?" Davy's voice was tense.

"I am." She flipped back through them all. "They are so similar, but there are differences. Can I write on these?"

"Use the back. That way, nothing will be lost." Davy watched as she rapidly noted the differences, leaning over to read them as she did. He nodded. She's good, isn't she? She's finding everything and more that I picked up.

Deri sat back finally, exhausted, her eyes on the photo that looked so much like her.

"What is going on? Are we the wrong targets?"

"That we are working on. I spoke with a superintendent of the London force. He was horrified to find out that your concerns had been shuffled to one side. He stated that should not have happened. He's looking into your claims, but says there is no documentation that he can find."

"I have report numbers that I can get you. We were given those. What did they do? Destroy them? Give us dummy numbers?"

"That will get sorted out, I am sure. But now? We need to identify these young ladies. You don't know them at all?"

Deri shook her head and then regretted it, a hand going to her temple. "Sorry. I shouldn't have done that." Pain lanced through her head for a moment. "No, I don't think that I do. You'll be contacting the others?"

"If I can. They all seem to have gone into hiding. One of our detectives is flying over there, to work with the detectives there. Any information that you can provide would be welcome."

"I don't think I can add anything. We never saw one another outside of the studio. I taught music at a local boarding school to help make ends meet. I couldn't begin to tell you what the others did."

"That's okay, Deri. You have given me information that will help move this along." Davy stood, his eyes on her. "I can't stress enough that you need to be careful. Monitor your emails, calls, and texts. Call me immediately if you have anything come through that worries you." He looked over at Dallas. "And that goes for you too, Dallas. You know the drill."

"I do, unfortunately. Thanks, Davy."

"I'm off. I'm certain that someone will give you a lift home, Dallas. If not, call me." Davy walked away, leaving the two in the kitchen staring after him and then at one another.

"What did he mean?"

"He gave me a lift here. He found me walking the downtown area."

"Bored?" Deri was on her feet, her eyes on the clock. "I'm on supper duty tonight. Just let me put the casserole in the oven and then I can make the salad." She moved quickly around the kitchen, finding Dallas finally standing in her way. "Dallas?"

"What can I do? I have one good hand. At least, it's my dominant hand." He grinned at her.

"You could set the table. We eat in here. Plates in that cupboard. I see that you found the utensil drawer."

"That I did." He moved away, pulling out plates and setting the table. "Deri? You're sure about those photos?"

She nodded. "I am. The differences are subtle and unless you knew the ladies, you would not see them." She paused, a sharp knife still in the air over the tomato that she had been slicing. "I wonder if they had plastic surgery to make them look like us."

"That's a possibility. I sure Davy will look into that." Dallas finally moved to take the knife from her hand and draw her into a hug. "I'm sorry, Deri. This shouldn't be happening to a beautiful young lady."

"Thank you, Dallas, but age and disputed beauty don't mean that things don't happen to us." She leaned back to look up at him. "What about you? Any thoughts on who it might be?"

"Davy and I talked before we came here. He's looking at the threats that I had." His finger laid on her lips stopped her words. "It happens, Deri. It's part of the job. Not a welcome part, but a part."

Chapter 14

Three days later, Dallas tucked the sling into his jacket pocket and headed for his car. He was free to drive again, as long as he didn't try any demo derbies, the surgeon said. He had healed well, better than had been expected. His steps slowed as he approached his vehicle and sighed. This is par for the course, isn't it, Lord? An envelope on my windshield. He leaned over to take a look before his phone was out and he was calling Davy.

Davy approached him with the same caution that Dallas had approached his car.

"Dallas?"

"There." Dallas simply pointed to the windshield. "A warning or something like that more than likely."

"I would think so. The first one that you'd received?" As Dallas nodded, Davy pulled on latex gloves and reached for the letter, pulling open the envelope and removing the letter. Before he unfolded it, he looked at Dallas.

"Let's see what there is, Davy."

Davy nodded, his hands unfolding it. "They're not very nice, Dallas."

"I didn't expect them to be." He stood and read the threat against his life. "This is brutal. But I don't

———

get the connection to that person that they mention. I don't recognize that name."

"And I know that you have a good memory for names." Davy tucked the envelope and letter into an evidence bag and noted the date and time, initialling it. "I'll run it and see what I can find." He looked towards the building. "Someone was following you."

"They had to be. I'm freed to drive again, by the way."

"That's good. I was worried about you walking everywhere." Davy stood for a moment. "I've been looking into those threats. All talk as far as I can determine. But someone is after you. I talked to one of my contacts on the streets. There are rumbles of that on the streets but nothing definite that anyone could tell me. You still need to be extremely careful."

"I will, Davy. I keep wracking my brain to come up with someone and just can't." Dallas leaned against his car.

"I know you are. I'm doing the same. I heard a lot on the streets but nothing really about you. For some reason, that didn't happen. And it always happens about the detectives." He leaned back on the car beside Dallas, his arms folding across his chest.

"I know the drill, as you say, Davy, but it's different when it's you. How do I do this?" Dallas sighed, his eyes on the blue of the sky. "I don't want harm to come to anyone."

"We know that, Dallas. Right now, you need to heal. Not just physically. I know the stress that you have been under. You need time to heal in all ways." Davy looked on with compassion as Dallas nodded. "Spend time with your lady. She'll help."

"I know, but how do I do that and still not bring danger to her." Dallas watched as Davy walked away before he drove off himself, heading home. He needed to spend time with the Lord and that wouldn't happen if he stayed standing on the street, now would it?

Hours later, he looked up as he heard a tap at the door and rose from where he had been kneeling by his couch. He stretched, stiff from not moving, before he headed for the door, peeking out and then opening the door.

"Devin? I thought that you were working today." Dallas knew that Devin as an investigative reporter had been out and about that day. Just what story he was working on, he wasn't sure.

"I am. You're my story, Dallas. I talked to my editor. We want to try and help you. I can't help Deri. She's too close to me. There would be bias." Devin took the mug of coffee offered to him. "You know, Deri used to enjoy her coffee. Living in London? She says the coffee is not the same there. That's why she has switched to tea."

"I can see that. I was there once years ago on holidays and found that. I attended a nice concert or two, one given by a number of young ladies." Dallas froze as he spoke, his face turning white. "Devin, can you ask your sister if she and her musician friends gave a concert on this date and at this place?" He stated the date and the venue.

<hr>

"I can tell you without asking that she did. It was one of the first that the group gave. It was organized by the studio that Deri was working with on her first album." Devin stopped, his eyes on Dallas as he digested his words. "There's our connection. Did no one ever ask if you had been in London?"

Dallas shook his head. "No, no one. Not even Davy." He rose, searching for the phone that he had tossed aside when he came home, sending off a text to Davy. "Maybe, just maybe we'll get somewhere now."

Chapter 15

Her mind on other things, Deri wandered the stores in the downtown area, looking up at the signs and then entering one. A little bookshop, nestled between a cafe and a clothing store, was a favourite of hers. She sighed. It was good to be home, but I miss the little shops in London. I could spend hours wandering through them.

She was searching for something, she just wasn't sure what. Christmas would soon be upon her. Her gifts for her family were wrapped and tucked away in a closet, but there was someone else to buy for this year. A smile softened her face. Dallas had either been by the house or called her every day. She looked forward to that, not sure that she should. She really had no idea where this was going. Deri feared for him, afraid that whoever it was after her would go after him. He told her it was the other way, that whoever was after him might go after her. Her question to him had stilled his voice. What if it is the same person, she asked? His response was how did they know that it was?

Hearing a voice beside her, she looked up, a smile coming to her face.

"Neasa? What are you doing here?" She reached to hug her cousin's wife. She studied her, glad that Breck had found his helpmeet. "You're up to something!"

Neasa grinned. "Shopping for Christmas. Same as you. Listen, do you have time for a coffee or an early lunch?"

Deri shrugged. She remembered Neasa from church and the youth group. She hadn't known her well, as she was older by a few years, but she had always admired her.

"I guess. Do you?" She looked past her as two other ladies their age approached. "You're not on your own."

"No, I'm not. Do you remember Buckley? This is his wife, Locklin. And this is Baird's wife, Berneen."

Deri smiled at them. "I saw them in church on Sunday. Sorry, ladies. There were just too many people who wanted to speak with me on Sunday. Old friends and church family, I guess. That's what happens when you leave town and then return."

"No problem, Deri." Berneen smiled. "So, are we up for lunch or still shopping?"

Deri opened her mouth to reply when she saw exactly what she wanted for Dallas. "Still shopping, I think. I just need to get this and then we can do lunch." She turned as she heard a soft laugh. "Aubrey?"

"I'm here too. At least it's not the fourteen of us." She laughed again as she saw Deri struggling to understand. "There are fourteen of us ladies in the Barnabas Foundation building. That includes Breck and Barnabas. And we have all had adventures, just like you." She tucked her arm into Deri's. "Now, let's get your purchase done. And just where do we go for lunch?"

"The diner next door." Deri looked around, worried that she had overstepped. "It's run by good friends of Mom and Dad's. I always eat there if I happen to be downtown at a mealtime."

"I love their food." Berneen headed for the door, Locklin following. "I'll find us a table and then you three join us."

Neasa watched them walk away before she looked back at Deri, finding her cousin staring down at the bag she held in her hand.

"Deri? You don't have to."

"I know. It's just that I'm so afraid that one of you will be hurt because of me. I don't know if I could live with that." Deri looked up, uncertainty on her face.

"As has been said, we've been there." Aubrey turned her towards the door. "This diner is used by the police in the area. There are always officers there. If someone sees us together, then we deal with it. I don't think that anyone will go after us. They never did in the past."

Neasa pulled the door open, her eyes on the man across the street who seemed intent on watching Deri. "Just a moment, ladies. I just need to send a text off to my brother." She took a photo of the man and sent it on to Davy who had requested that personally of each one of Breck's friends.

Once they were seated, their orders placed, Neasa turned to Deri, holding out her phone.

"Do you know this man? He seemed to be watching you."

Deri shot her a startled look before she stared at the photo.

"No, I don't. At least I don't think I do. Can you forward that to me, Neasa? And to Dallas?"

Neasa did that and then the conversation turned to other things. Deri sat, for the most part, quiet and just observing the ladies. Neasa watched her as did Aubrey and the two ladies exchanged glances. There was more going on, Neasa thought, than just this. She came home for more than that.

Chapter 16

Dallas stared down at the photo that Neasa had forwarded to him, a frown on his face. No, he thought, he didn't know this person. Lord? Is he the one behind this? I know. I'm talking to You again, aren't I? Life got between us and that should never have happened. I just wish it hadn't taken this to do this. Please, dear Lord? Protect my Deri. Don't let harm come to her. I have no idea where we're going but You do.

Hearing the doorbell ring, Dallas sighed. He wasn't in the mood for company, not today. Today was the anniversary of his parents' and sister's death and he usually spent it by himself, hiding from his brother and sister and everyone else. His phone hit the countertop as he headed for the door.

Peeking out, he frowned. Susan? Why was she here?

"Susan?" Dallas' voice had Susan spinning around to face him. He drew in a breath. She looks devastated, Lord. "Come in."

Susan stepped hesitantly in, her jacket sliding from her hand before she reached for him.

"Dallas, I'm sorry. And I just need one of your big brother hugs."

Dallas hugged her, a frown still in place. What was she saying?"

"Susan?" He stepped back, his eyes watchful.

"Can we talk, Dallas? I mean really talk. I have been so horrible for so many years. The Lord finally got through to me." Tears sparkled on her cheeks, tears that he had not seen her cry in years.

"Sure. Come on through to the kitchen."

They sat and chatted over mundane things before Susan pulled out her phone.

"I got this last night, too late to call you. I don't know what it means." She handed over the phone.

Dallas stared down at the photo and read the accompanying text.

"With your permission, I want to forward it to myself and also to Davy, the detective that is working this case." He didn't want to see her nod but instead forwarded the photo. "How did they get your number?"

"It's not hard, Dallas. I have business cards out there, advertising my work. You know that. Anyone could have been into the studio and picked on up. Or even searched online. Is this what you meant when you told me to be careful?"

"It is, Susan. They know who you two are, likely from you being here when I was in the hospital. Have you spoken with Sean?"

"I tried. He was heading into a meeting that he couldn't delay. Something about some takeover."

"Takeover? What's that?" Dallas searched her face. "The business?"

"That's right. They're taking over a small manufacturing company and Sean has been the one doing the negotiations. Today was the day that they were working through all of the small details."

"I see. I know he said that it was coming up. It's not a good day for that."

"No, it's not. I am so sorry, Dallas. I was angry with Mom about something trivial, some outfit that she wanted me to wear. I didn't want to and had been pouting for days about it. Now, it seems so senseless. I can't even ask her to forgive me."

"But you can ask God." Dallas hugged his sister, his prayer for her whispered in her ear. "Now, how many bookings do you have between now and Christmas?"

"Very few, if you must know. I have been doing more studio work of my own, launching that line, getting out of the portraits, other than for animals." She looked up. "I get tired of trying to get people to pose."

Dallas began to laugh. "You used to do that to us. Make us pose so that you could practice."

Susan grinned. "I did. And when you and Deri marry, I'm your photographer."

"Who said anything about us getting married?" He reached for his phone, his laughter dying. "Susan? Did you leave your business locked? And is there anything there that you can't replace?"

"Not really. I back all my photos up to the cloud. I have moved all my equipment home as well as the computers. It was empty really. I had put in my notice that I was vacating the premises and that is up at the end of the month. Why?"

"Because Davy has been asked to look for you. Your studio went up in flames not too long ago."

Susan paled and then reached for her phone. "I muted it last night and forgot to unmute it. Oh, no! They were trying to reach me."

"Call them back. I'll see if we need to head that way today."

Dallas was on his feet, his own phone out, calling Davy.

"Davy?"

"Dallas. Your sister? Where is she?" He could hear the urgency in Davy's voice.

"With me. She received that threat last night and then headed here this morning. And before you ask, Sean is in a daylong meeting."

"Good. Keep your sister there. They don't want her to come back. Not until they have more information. It was arson, Dallas. And they need to investigate that. She's in danger as well. Let me call Sean and make sure that he is aware of this and that he will be under protection as of now. They've been linked to you and now are threatened. That's the word that I just got from my street sources."

"I understand. I'll keep her here if I can. She said that she had cleared out her studio in the last little while, planning on just doing her own photography." Dallas paused, a thought striking him. "Deri?"

"She's at lunch right now with Neasa, Aubrey, and a couple of the other ladies. I'll bring her to you or to her home. She was walking. Do you understand that, Dallas? She was on foot."

"On foot? Deri!"

Chapter 17

Deri looked up, laughter on her face that died away as she saw Davy walking towards her. She excused herself and rose to meet him.

"Davy? I don't like that look."

"No, you won't. Susan's studios just went up in flames. Sean is going into protection. And you, young lady, are walking. What part of it don't you understand?"

"I'm sorry? I'm not to be walking? That's how I get around." Deri wasn't sure what Davy meant.

"And that makes you a perfect target. They could nab you and be gone and we would have no idea where you were taken from. At least, if you're in a car, you have a chance to escape. Or we can find your car and track you from here." Davy watched as she paled, not willing to let her get away with shrugging it off. "This is serious business, Deri. Now, are you through with your lunch? I can wait if you're not."

"No. No, I am. We were just talking." She turned, her white face shocking the other ladies as she approached them. "I'm sorry, ladies. It looks as if I need to leave. I didn't mean to break up our lunch." She dropped some money on the table for her meal. "Please? Neasa, call me later?"

"That I will. Off with Davy now, Deri. We'll do this again. And one day we'll find all the ladies and do that. And we have a Bible study meeting on Monday afternoons if you want to join us. We rotate between our homes.”

The four ladies watched her walk away, Davy’s hand to the small of her back as he directed her towards his vehicle.

“She’s hurting, ladies.” Berneen commented. “She’s like we were. Only she doesn’t have the support of a fellow in her life to help.”

“She does, Berneen. Dallas has made that obvious. He’s just going slow with her. She’s trying to reacclimatize herself to Canada again after living in London.” Neasa studied her friends. “Breck is concerned about the two of them. I must say that I am as well.”

“We know, Neasa.” Aubrey dug out the money to pay for her own meal. “Did you say that she taught music?”

“That’s what Breck said. She taught in a boarding school.” Neasa stared at her friend and then her face brightened. “She’s who you need in your music program.”

“She is, but I don’t know that she’s ready to do that. We’ll pray about it, shall we?” Aubrey rose, heading off with the checks and the money to pay for their meals.

Dallas stood watching Deri as she roamed his living room. Susan was in his office, talking with the police and then the fire officials. She had contacted the landlord and was relieved that he was more concerned about her than about the building. Even if it was arson, he was glad that she had not been in there.

"Deri?" Dallas finally moved into her path and reached out to steady her. "What happened?"

"Did you get that photo Neasa sent on?" She looked up at him, fear in her eyes.

"I did. He was watching you, she said."

"He was. Davy tracked me down. He told me off for walking. It's how I travel, Dallas. It's what I've done for so many years. That or the double-decker bus or the tube." She referred to the modes of transportation in London, Dallas understanding that in Canada the tube would be called the subway.

"I know, love, but we need to keep you safe. You have a driver's license?"

"I do. I kept it up over the years." She frowned. "But I don't have a vehicle. Dad and Mom both use theirs. So does Devin."

"I can take you car shopping if you would like." Dallas grinned at her. "At least, I would if you will let me."

Deri shrugged, even as she studied his face, a frown on hers as she read something in his eyes that she had longed to see in a man's eyes but not at a time such as this. A something that said she was beautiful and that she was his.

"I guess. I'm just not sure about this. I have lyrics that I need to compose." Frustrated, she pulled out her phone as it kept vibrating. "Excuse me, Dallas. I really do need to take this. Elizabeth? You're calling? What happened?"

Dallas watched as she sank down onto the couch, reaching for the pad of paper and pen he had on the end table. He headed for the kitchen, squinting at the clock. It was mid-afternoon and he realized that neither he nor Susan had had their lunch. His head turned as he heard soft footsteps.

"Susan?"

She looked up at him, brushing away the frown on her face. "It's okay. I've talked to everyone that I need to right now. I may have to head home, but the police detective thinks that I should stay away from town for a bit. But I need my things. My computer. My backups."

"Let me have a list of what you want, where we would find it, and your keys. Some of the fellows will gladly head that way. I know some of my fellow officers will. They have offered to help in any way that they can. Davy expressed that to me."

"Oh, that would be wonderful. Except I don't have a place to live."

"You can stay here or I can ask Breck if there is an apartment in the Foundation building that you can use." He held up a hand. "There are extra apartments there that can be used for circumstances such as yours." He looked past her. "Deri's here."

"She is? Wonderful. I can apologize to her today." Susan turned, stopping as Dallas' hand was laid on her arm.

"Not now, Susan. She's on a business call."

"She is? Oh, okay. Lunch! We didn't eat."

Dallas grinned. "No, we didn't. I was making us a sandwich when you came in. Sit and eat yours. I need to see if Deri wants anything."

Chapter 18

A week later, Dallas stood in the Curran kitchen, waiting for Deri to appear. It was the afternoon that the Foundation building family had decided to have their Christmas get-together, a first for the building. Brock's worship team from the church had been asked to provide music over the afternoon. Dallas grinned to himself as he remembered the blank look on his face as Bruce had asked, a smile on his face, before Brock agreed only if Bruce would dust off his guitar and join them. Bruce had laughed and said it already was.

Deri appeared, suddenly unsure of herself. Dallas had asked if she would go with him. She had looked up at him and then grinned, asking if it was their first date. Dallas had been taken aback before he too grinned and responded that if she would go with him to that, then he would take her out on a real date. She had simply shaken a finger at him and agreed.

Neither had talked much with the other about what was going on. Deri was unsure how much information Dallas had been given. She had been given a report, asked to go over it and then return it with her comments to Davy. He had shaken his head at her protest and told her that she had information that they needed. Would she just please cooperate with him?

Turning as he heard Deri, Dallas paused before he handed her the roses he had in his hands. She smiled and found a vase for them. *I could get used to this,* she thought, but the danger we are in is too close. I can't depend on anyone but myself and the Lord. That thought had caused her to pause. No, she thought. I have to depend on others and that scares me.

Entering the lobby of the Foundation building, Deri stopped, joy on her face as she looked around.

"This is so beautiful. It's been years since I've been out here. I can see Elizabeth's hand in it."

"Hers and the ladies who live here. With today, Blair's Devaney headed the ladies' group to arrange this. I would say that this is wonderful, wouldn't you?"

"I would." She turned in a circle as he headed to hang up their jackets. "Dallas? Who all is here?"

"Just the building families. If the ladies had relatives, they are here as well. The board and their families. It makes for a big crowd, but not everyone will stay for the whole time. The board and their families are here for now but I understand that there are other events that they need to be at."

"Oh. Are we safe to be around them?" She looked up as he grinned. "Dallas!"

"We are, love. We are. Don't forget that each one of these couples had their own adventures." Dallas stood beside her for a moment. "Have you met everyone?"

"No, I'm not sure that I have. The men I have through Breck and Barnabas." She looked around as she heard children's voices. "Oh, there are little ones!"

"There are. The oldest are Brandon and Hagen's twins, Heath and Hannah. They are a pair, let me tell you. One thinks of what the other doesn't."

"Sounds busy." She took the glass of juice offered to her with a quiet thanks and then looked around some more. "Dad's here?"

"He is. Near the security desk. They brought in a small piano that I understand was in the music room that Aubrey has for the children and others. She's working on setting that up. There were also drums that your uncle approved of. Devin has his saxophone. Your mother has her viola. Bruce his guitar. Bonnie is involved too."

"She was in the old worship team. She had a tambourine and other assorted instruments like that. We always had a fun time. Barnabas was involved too." She turned as she felt an arm come around her shoulder. "Bruce. This is wonderful."

"It is. And this year, it's more so because you are here. Ready to do a couple of songs for us?"

Deri blushed before she nodded. "I guess. I'm trying to stay low key, you know."

Bruce laughed. "I know, but I think you're okay today. I'll call you up when we're ready."

Dallas and Deri mingled with his friends, Deri finding that she was welcomed. She caught a couple of older teenaged girls watching her, excitement on their faces and sighed. It's happening here too, isn't it, Lord? I want to anonymous right now, with everything going on and I can't.

——

86

Dallas had noticed the twins' interest and grinned.

"I think that you have a couple of fans here."

She sounded disgruntled as she replied. "I know. I have to meet them, I guess, but right now, I can see Uncle Beck looking for me. Excuse me, Dallas. This may not take that long." She smiled at him but he could see the uncertainty in her eyes.

"Just pretend that we're all friends, and we are. I for one am looking forward to hearing you sing." He followed her as she approached the musicians, leaning against the banister of the stairs so that he could watch her.

Beck spoke with Deri for a moment, concern on his face before he laughed and sent her off to sit on the piano bench beside her father. He turned to the group, noting that they were all eager to sing.

"Okay, folks. We'll do some that we have picked out. Deri has agreed to sing a couple of tunes for us. I'm looking forward to that."

Chapter 19

Deri's sweet soprano filled the lobby as she sang the songs that her uncle and her father had requested before she shook her head at her uncle.

"No more, Uncle Beck. Let them have their chance to make requests." She rose and slipped away from the piano, finding Dallas and then standing back to him, his arms wrapped around her. Neither one saw the speculative glances thrown their way.

"Those were your songs that you sang." Dallas had no doubt about that.

"They were. They're on my new album, which went out last week. I had to wait for that." She stared down at the little fellow who was leaning against her, a hand going out to rest on his head. "Who's this?"

"This is Heath. Watch out. He'll want up." Dallas grinned at her.

"He will, will he?" Deri grinned at Heath's little arms went up. "You want up?"

"Yeah. Up knee." Heath grinned, showing the little teeth that had come through before he hugged Deri and then smothered her in kisses.

Dallas was laughing even as Hagen's shocked voice said her son's name and she reached for him.

Deri shook her head. "It's okay. I don't mind." She watched with interest as Dallas picked up Heath's sister, Hannah. "And this must be Hannah. Am I correct?"

"You are." Dallas was content to stand beside her, listening as she sang.

Heath's little hands went to Deri's face, turning her to face him. A frown was on his face.

"Noise!"

"Noise?" Deri was confused before she grinned at the little one. "Yes. I do make noise when I sing. Do you?"

A little shoulder went up as Heath shrugged before he had pried open her mouth and had his eye close to it, peering in, intent on finding where the noise was coming from.

"Heath! You don't do that!" Hagen once more reached for her son, who clung to Deri.

Deri shook her head at Hagen. "I don't mind. I have had worse directed at me by little ones not much older than he is." She turned back to Heath. "Let me see. Do you have noise as well?" Heath's little mouth was open so Deri could inspect it. "Yep. You've got noise in there too." She turned as she felt Hannah reaching for her.

"Me. Me too. Me have noise?" Hannah clung to Deri, not letting Dallas take her back.

Dallas was having a hard time controlling his laughter and he saw the strangled look on Brandon's face as well as he watched his twins, barely able to contain his own laughter.

—

Deri inspected Hannah's mouth as well before she nodded. "Yep. You have noise too. A pretty noise." She turned as Heath's hand hit her face.

"Me. Pretty noise."

"Oh, no, Heath. You are a boy. You have handsome noise. Hannah's a girl. She has pretty noise."

That seemed to satisfy the two and Deri's attention went back to the band as the requests continued, her body swaying gently with the music.

Bradon finally spoke. "I have a song that I love to hear at Christmas, but I have never heard it sung at church. About the holy night."

Beck nodded from where he still sat at the drums.

"No, we haven't had it sung there. Our members just won't have it. You see, Breck, Barnabas, and Deri used to do it for years as a trio. We all felt that we didn't want to hear anyone else sing it." He shared a look with Brock and then Bruce. "Deri, I'm going to put you, Breck, and Barnabas on the spot. Will you do it for us? We have all felt that we have been missing something at Christmas and that is you three on this song."

Deri simply handed the twins back to their parents, much to their dismay, and headed for the front, Breck and Barnabas walking step in step with her. Brock looked at them and then grinned.

"We don't need Barnabas' jacket, I take it." There was laughter from those who knew what he meant, even as Deri shook her head. "For those who don't know, I think it was when these three were about fifteen. Deri tried to slide down in the pew one Sunday because she wasn't feeling great and didn't want to sing. Barnabas handed Breck his jacket and helpful Breck tried to hide her. It didn't work very well. That is something that we can all relate to, I think. Deri, you don't know how glad we are to have you back home."

The building family listened in wonder as the three sang, taking turns in the verses as they had been wont to do in the past, with two stepping back as one sang and then stepping forward as they joined in. It was as if they had just sung the song the day before. Deri's sweet soprano melded with Breck's tenor and Barnabas' baritone, their arms around each other as they had always done, three friends who had been reunited. Brock listened closely, thinking that their voices were even more powerful as adults than they had been as teens. There was silence when they finished, the family seeming to see the night as it happened. Deri hugged the two men and walked back to Dallas and into his hug.

Chapter 20

Two days later, Dallas looked up at the hammering on his door and sighed. He was trying to study the book of James in the Bible and didn't really want any company. Susan had headed home, feeling that she needed to. She hadn't said when she would return. Deri was involved in composing a song that was needed soon and he didn't expect it to be her.

He stood, watching the man who was on his front porch, shifting from foot to foot.

"Can I help you?" Dallas kept a grip on the door, ready to slam it shut if he needed to.

"Sure. I'm looking for someone. A man by the name of Ben. This is his address. You Ben?" The foul smell of stale tobacco and coffee on the man's breath wafted towards Dallas.

"Sorry. Wrong address. There's no Ben here." He started to shut the door, unprepared for the attack that the man launched at it, slamming the door into Dallas and sending him flying backwards to the floor.

Dallas lay still for a moment, stunned before he felt himself hauled to his feet and shoved towards the door. He fought to get away but the man's grip was too strong. A second man met them at the foot of the stairs, his hand out to grasp Dallas' arm and shove him towards a vehicle. Pushed into it, Dallas spun on the seat, stopping and his hands raising as he saw the weapon pointed at him.

"What do you want?" When he received no response, he repeated his question. He groaned to himself as his wrists were bound with a rough rope, the rope pulled tight enough so that he knew he would be unable to release them.

He watched as they seemed to drive aimlessly around the town before a blindfold was suddenly dropped over his eyes. He cried out in surprise and protest, feeling the weapon jabbing at his side and stopping his words. He was finally forced from the vehicle, feeling the gravel under his socked feet. He had not been given a chance to put on shoes. And he shivered slightly without a jacket. He was shoved into a house and he felt a welcome warmth before he was pushed down into a chair. No words were exchanged with him and he could not hear what the men were discussing in another room.

Sometime later, Deri stood at the open door, calling for Dallas. She stepped back, a puzzled frown on her face as she saw his car in the driveway. She stood for a moment, hesitant to enter before she pulled out her phone.

"Davy?"

"Deri? I wasn't expecting to hear from you today. You have something more to add to the questionnaire." Davy sounded distracted, Deri's call pulling him from a case file that he was studying.

Deri could hear his chair squeaking in protest as he leaned backwards before her words were tumbling over one another.

"I'm at Dallas'. His car is here but the front door is wide open. I haven't gone in." She turned to stare back through the door. "This is stupid. He has to be here somewhere."

Davy was on his feet, running for the parking lot at the back of the detachment, his shouted words causing a scurry among the personnel in the building.

"Deri? Are you driving?" When she responded that she was, he drew a deep breath of relief. "Get yourself in your vehicle and drive away. Lock your doors. Head for here. I'm on my way there."

"Davy? I can't go in?" Deri hesitated, one foot raised to step forward.

"NO!" His word was almost shouted at her. "Run from there. Now!" Davy threw his phone on the seat beside him, the siren blaring and the lights flashing as he sped towards Dallas' home.

Davy didn't see Deri's car when he got there and breathed a sigh of relief. She's gotten away. Hopefully, she'll be at the detachment when I get back.

With his back up behind him, Davy moved slowly through Dallas' home, his weapon drawn and pointed downwards. Finally stepping back outside, he holstered his weapon and turned to the other responding officers.

"He's not here. And that's not like him to leave his door open."

"No, it's not." The officer was a good friend of Dallas. "He's very careful that way. I called for the crime scene techs."

"Good." Davy searched the area with his eyes. "Spread out. Talk to the neighbours. See if anyone was home and saw anything."

Two hours later, he finally walked back into the detachment, fatigue drawing at him. There had been no sign of Dallas and no evidence to show what had happened. That worried him. Davy looked around the front of the building, turning at long last to the desk officer.

"Deri Curran? Where is she?"

"Deri? She's not here. Not all afternoon. Was she to be?" He looked up from the reports that he was working on.

"She was. I sent her here when I headed out for Dallas' home." Davy was worried, heading for his office. His phone out, he turned it over and over, not wanting to make the call that he had to. "Beth? Is Deri there? I need to speak with her."

"Deri?" Beth turned from where she had been looking out the window, her phone in her hand. "No. She left a note that she was heading for downtown and then to see Dallas." When silence greeted her words, her heart fell. "Davy?"

"She's not there? She had been at Dallas' and found his door open. I sent her to the detachment on my way there. She's not here."

—

"She would have waited for you." Beth looked up as Brock entered. "Brock? Have you seen Deri?"

"No. She was to be home for most of the day, she told me. Something about a tune she was working on." Brock paused in his movements to hang up his jacket. "What happened?"

"Davy is on the phone. She was at Dallas' and there was something wrong. He sent her to the station, only she's not there."

Brock's face paled even as he pulled on his jacket once more, turning to find Devin standing behind him.

"Deri's missing. Head out, Devin. We're searching."

Chapter 21

Davy stood in the Curran kitchen, a mug of coffee in his hand even as he bit into the sandwich that Bonnie had simply handed him. They had searched, even the officers on patrol, but not one of them had found Deri or even her vehicle. That this worried him was an understatement. Where is she? Lord, You and I have been off talking terms for a number of years. These two young people are bringing me back, to help me return to You. I could sure use a favour about now. I know, it's not a favour, but a request. Excuse the phrasing I use. I'm just not used to speaking with You, Lord. Help us to find them.

Brock turned from where he had been speaking with their minister, Daniel, and came to stand beside him, reaching for a sandwich as well. He looked down at it with distaste, not wanting to eat but knowing that he had to.

"Anything, Davy?" His heart sank as Davy shook his head.

"Not a thing. There is no sign of her. No sign of her car. The techs went back to the house and went over the street again. Officers have spoken with the neighbours. No evidence. No signs of anything out of the ordinary."

"And there should be. There is always one neighbour who sees everything." He looked up as Breck and Beck appeared.

"Brock?" Beck spoke, eyeing the others in the kitchen. "What's happening? We've been out of town today."

"Dallas and Deri are missing. Disappeared some time this afternoon from Dallas' home." Brock sagged back against the counter. "We've been out looking and haven't found her."

Breck exchanged a look with his father and then moved away, his phone out.

"Barnabas? What are the fellows up to tomorrow?" Breck didn't even waste any time greeting his friend.

"At work, I would suspect. Why?" Breck could hear the water running in his friend's kitchen and knew that he had caught them just as they finished their meals.

"Dallas and Deri have disappeared. I wondered if the men would be willing to help search tomorrow."

"Absolutely. You're at Brock's?" Barnabas turned as Aubrey approached him, a question on her face. "I'll send out a group text. Aubrey and I will there as soon as we can."

"Barnabas?" Aubrey walked into his hug.

"Dallas and Deri are missing. I'm sending out the group text to the guys. Can you do the same for the ladies? And then I'll need to call Dad."

"You look after what you need to. I'll do the ladies and then Dad."

Barnabas stood in the doorway, watching his friend and his family. The worry was there, he could see. Bonnie had her arm around Beth, trying to bring what comfort she could to the frightened woman. Elizabeth had moved to stand beside them, and he could tell that his mother was praying. He approached Davy.

"Davy?"

"Barnabas? You're here. Of course, you would be." Davy gave a grim smile. "The men heading out in the morning."

"They are. Someone has called Sean and Susan?"

Davy nodded. "I have officers in that town doing that. We don't want them here, not yet."

"What happened?"

"That we don't know." Davy watched Breck and Devin as they had moved into his space. "Devin, did Deri say anything today?"

"Nothing. Not about that. She was focused on the song she was working on. She was just finishing it. Polishing it as she put it. I looked at her notes. She had done that and likely emailed it on to whoever it was for. She doesn't talk about her clients."

"No, she shouldn't." Davy rubbed at the back of his neck. "I have officers here setting up a system that if a ransom call comes in, we're ready to trace it. Even if it comes in as a text."

"Thank you, Davy." Brock laid a hand on the younger man's shoulder. "You're doing what you can. We appreciate that. I doubt any of us will be sleeping, but there are blankets and pillows piled up in the family room. Air mattresses as well. Or there is a bedroom upstairs that can be used."

Chapter 22

Two days went by. Davy had been in and out of the Curran house as had the building men. No one had found any evidence of the two. That frustrated Davy. He had gone to his sources on the street and found no answer or information there. The people had nodded, confirmed with him that they were looking but hadn't found the couple.

Then, Davy gave a shout as he pocketed his phone. He had returned to the office. The officers and civilians in the building jumped and then approached him.

"Come on, whoever it is that can. I have a location. We need to move and move now before they disappear from there."

Davy pulled to a stop a block from the address he had been given and was out of his vehicle, popping open his trunk and retrieving his body armour. He had no doubt that there was danger involved in this rescue.

"How do you want to work this, Davy?" The most senior patrol officer on the scene stood beside him.

"The emergency response team? They're here."

"They are and ready to go in when you give the word."

"Okay. Let me find them and send them in. Then, we follow once they've cleared the area." He looked around. "Paramedics?"

"We have two units here. Brady and Patrick are one of them." Brady was one of the building fellows and a good friend to Dallas.

"They are? Okay. Let's get moving, people. Set up your perimeter."

"Already done. I didn't have to ask. They just moved in and did it."

Davy waited impatiently and anxiously as he watched the ETF members move towards the house and then in through the front and back doors. Lord? You promised me. You told me that we would find them. Please, Lord? It's almost Christmas. Let them be there and okay.

He looked up as one of the officers ran towards him and he moved forward.

"Jim?"

"We have them, Davy. We just need to clear the area. There's a suspicious package in there. Tim wants the bomb squad to see if we can move them out right away."

"Go." Davy turned towards the paramedics. "Okay, fellows. We move in and move out as quickly as we can. Do a fast assessment and save the long one for once they're out."

Brady and Patrick looked at one another, Brady's heart dropping.

"A bomb?" His voice was low as he spoke to Patrick.

"Something like that, I suspect. They don't say that unless there is." Patrick stood with his hand on the stretcher before he began to dig out the equipment that they would need for the fast assessment. "You heard him, fellows. A quick in and out. Brady and I will take Dallas. You two are on Deri."

"Deri?" Drew looked up. "Deri Curran?"

"That's right, Drew." Patrick paused. "You were in school with her."

"I was. And my wife loves her music." His face grew grim. "Okay, Tom. We're ready when they give the word."

As soon as they had word that it was clear, the four moved in. A quick assessment as they were asked and they were moving the two from the building. Brady stared down at his friend's white face that was covered in cuts and bruises as he was laid on one of the stretchers. Drew had carried Deri out, his face stern as he studied his friend's face.

"He's been beaten."

"He has. Likely as he was trying to get to Deri." Patrick looked up as he heard an exclamation from Tom. "Tom?"

"She has at least one broken finger, every bone. And it was no accident." Drew looked up. "We're ready to roll."

Davy stood near them. "Go. I'm on the calls to the family." He watched as the stretchers were wheeled quickly away before he turned at a call from the bomb squad leader.

"Paul?" Davy stood, seeing the urgency with which Paul was approaching him.

"Evacuate now. Thank goodness this is a building not close to any other. The bomb has been triggered and I don't have the time to defuse it."

Davy nodded, a shout going out to all the officers, who ran for their vehicles and drove away, to stop and turn to watch the building. In his vehicle, Davy felt the repercussion of the blast, watching in wonder as the building simply collapsed on itself. It was too close, Lord. Just too close. I'd be thanking You, Lord, that You led us to them so that we could get them out.

Chapter 23

Hand in hand, Brock and Beth almost ran into the Emergency Department, heading for the clerk's desk. The clerk had looked up, a smile of sympathy on her face before she motioned to the waiting room.

Brock seated Beth and then began to pace, his eyes on the doors that they were not allowed through yet. Devin appeared, hugging his mother, questions on his lips that she could not answer. Breck appeared shortly after, to pace with his uncle, knowing that his father would have been there if he could have been.

The building family trickled in and out over the hour that they waited. Barnabas and Aubrey had simply stayed, Barnabas knowing that he would likely be needed. He looked up as the physician on duty called for him and Breck.

"Barnabas. Breck." The physician simply pointed to the door he was holding open. "Come on it. I talked to Dallas' sister and brother. They have asked that I speak with you. They have authorized any treatment that we need to do, but they want someone here to speak with us. That would be you two."

Breck nodded. "How is he?"

"Beaten and beaten badly. He looks as if he struggled to get away and paid the price."

"He would. If Deri was in danger, then he would have tried to get to her, to help her." Barnabas stared down at his friend. "What are we looking at?"

"A lot of bruising. No internal bleeding. No fractures that we can see on imaging." The physician stood back. "He's dehydrated and we're working on rehydrating him. Any questions?"

"For treatment, rest, ice packs, pain medications?" Breck looked at the physician, who was nodding.

"That's about it. It will take time to heal. Find whoever it was that did this. If they get their hands on him again, he might not survive. I've seen that in the big cities where I work." He walked away, leaving the two friends staring after him.

"He's right, you know." Barnabas was frustrated. "And we are no closer to finding out who it was."

"No, I don't think we are. Dallas hadn't mentioned getting any of the usual, the photos, the texts, the voice mails. But then he has an unlisted number."

"He does and he doesn't give it out readily." Barnabas paced. "I'll go and update our friends. Are you calling Susan and Sean?"

"I can. At some point. Right now, I want to speak with Davy."

"And you will." Barnabas stood for a moment, his eyes on Dallas as his friend began to rouse. "Dallas?"

"Barnabas? What? Where am I?" Dallas was confused, his blurry eyes searching the room.

"In the hospital, my friend." Barnabas watched closely, seeing the moment that Dallas did realize where he was.

"They found me. Deri?" He roused enough again to ask about her.

"She's here, too. I don't know how she is."

"She's been hurt. I tried to stop them. They wanted her to agree to something. I'm not sure what. I couldn't understand it. She refused." Dallas slipped away, this time to a natural sleep.

The physician had paused inside the door as Dallas spoke before he moved forward.

"He's been awake. That's good." He watched for a moment, assessing Dallas' vital signs. "We can likely let him go home today. Has he someone with him?"

"No, but I imagine Brock and Beth will take him to their home. Deri?"

"She's under the care of another physician. He's speaking with her parents now, I think." His hand rested on Barnabas' shoulder. "Your friend was lucky."

"No luck, Doctor. God."

"God? He's here in this? I don't see that." The physician shook his head, thinking back to the faith his mother had tried to install in him.

"He was there. If He hadn't been, they wouldn't be here. The bomb that was in the building brought the building down just after they were removed."

The physician stared at him for a moment before he shook his head. "Whatever." But in his mind, he wondered if God really had been there.

Chapter 24

Brock and Beth stared in horror at the physician who was describing Deri's injuries. They were not sure that they had heard him correctly. Brock glanced at his wife before he spoke.

"A broken finger?"

"That's correct, Brock." Doc Whitson stared at him before he shook his head. "It was deliberate. Her baby finger on her left hand. All three bones."

Beth shut her eyes, not willing to even imagine how that had hurt.

"Why?" Her voice was a whisper.

"That I can't answer you. The orthopedic surgeon has been in to see her. He says that they are clean breaks and he has set them. She'll need to wear the buddy splint for a number of weeks." Doc held up his hand at Beth's protest. "I know what she does, Beth. But for now, the splint is on. If it isn't, the finger will heal deformed and that will affect her future."

"I see." Brock's eyes turned to where Deri lay, sleeping, an IV line in place to rehydrate, just as it was with Dallas. "What else?"

"She has some facial bruising. A split lip. Dehydration. The shock from the pain." Doc turned to watch Deri as well. "She's fortunate, Brock, Beth. It could have been a lot worse. Davy's been around. He'll be speaking with you both." Doc walked away, leaving Deri's parents to approach the stretcher.

Beth's hand went out to brush the tangled curls from her daughter's face before she looked up at Brock, seeing the anger rising in him.

"Let God have your anger, love."

"I know. But it still angers me that someone did this. And I spoke with Davy just before we came in. He called. He says the building that they were found in was destroyed by a bomb."

Beth paled. "A bomb? When?"

"Apparently just after they were removed. The bomb squad leader told him that they didn't have time to defuse it." Brock's hand rested on his daughter's for a moment. "Listen. I'm heading out and will send Devin in. I'll talk to Beck and Bonnie and the others." He hugged his wife and disappeared, Devin appearing in just minutes.

Beck walked towards his brother, seeing the distress on his face.

"Brock? Walk with me." Beck saw Breck approaching. "What did the physician say?"

"Doc. Bruising, on her face. Dehydration." Brock struggled to control his emotions. "Her baby finger was broken. All three bones."

"All three?" Beck stared at him. "How?"

"Deliberate, I'm told. They tortured her, Beck." Brock was unable to control the tears. "They

———

110

deliberately hurt my baby girl. What did they want from her?"

Beck's arm was around his brother's shoulders even as he prayed for him. Breck had to struggle to control his anger.

"Dad?" Breck caught his father's attention when he had finished praying.

"Find Davy. I want to speak with him." Brock spoke before Beck could say anything. "I want to know where the investigation stands."

Davy had been watching the men before he approached them. He didn't have news that he could share. The building would have to be moved with heavy equipment but he doubted that they would find much evidence in it. Not with the destruction and resulting fire. The fire chief had been around to speak with him, concerned about the couple.

Brock looked up as he heard footsteps, his eyes on Davy.

"Davy? What can you tell us?"

"Not a lot. I'm sorry, Brock. I got the message that was where they were. We went in, got them out, and then the building came down."

"Any idea who?" Breck shared a look with his father. He knew too well that feeling of helplessness.

"No. Not yet. My street sources are scrambling for me, trying to find out who. So far, we have nothing. Again, I'm sorry, Brock." Davy had no words to really express how he felt.

"I know, Davy. I know." Brock hesitated. "At least we have them and have them safe. For now. How do we keep them that way?"

"I don't know, Brock. We can't lock them away. Neither one would stand for that." He shared a look with Breck. "Breck, I know you have friends who would step in. For now, let's not. I need to speak with both of them before we make any plans."

Brock nodded. "I know that, Davy. Just how do we do this? How do we keep them safe? Dallas is part of the family. I am assuming that Susan and Sean are safe."

"They are. We have ensured that." Davy looked past him towards the examination rooms. "Is Deri awake?"

"She hadn't been. I can go see." Brock stood, his feet seemingly unable to move.

"It's okay, Brock. I'll head on back. I need to see to Dallas anyway." Davy walked away from the men, finding his own anger building and asking the Lord that he had returned to that He would remove it and help him to find the ones responsible.

Chapter 25

Rousing, Dallas stared around at the room that he was in, confused as to his location. He sighed. Lord, what happened? I don't remember much, but I hurt. A lot. And all over. Really hurt on my face. He reached to touch it, wincing as he did so, finding the bruises and the odd cut. His shoulder that had been wounded stung with pain as he moved.

Davy watched him from where he had been seated, his laptop open on his knee as he worked away. It was late at night and the nurse had assured him that he could stay. He set aside the computer and rose, to stand beside Dallas, a hand on the younger man's arm.

"Dallas?"

Dallas groaned as he moved, his eyes squinting in the low light.

"Davy? Do they have you too?"

Davy gave a grim smile. "No, Dallas. You're free. We were able to find you two and get you to safety. What can you tell me?"

Dallas sighed. "Not letting me get away with anything, are you? I can't tell you much other than a man was at my door asking for someone. He then attacked me, dragged me out of my house, shoved me into a car, and then drove me around for a long time." He peered at Davy. "Deri? Is she here?"

"She is. She's asleep right now, just down the hall from you." Davy noted down what Dallas had said. "I'll have to get a formal statement from you. Are you up to it now?"

Dallas nodded. "I guess. Then it's done with." He detailed all that he could before he paused, a frown on his face. "I don't get what they wanted. I wasn't asked anything at all."

"Deri. They were using you to get Deri to cooperate with them. It doesn't look as if it worked too well."

Dallas stared at Davy. "What aren't you telling me? Deri? How is she?"

"She's sleeping right now. Like you, she was dehydrated. Beaten to some extent. It's the broken finger that we're concerned about."

"Broken finger? How? I don't remember seeing her fall or anything." He stared at Davy before his head went back, his eyes closing as he gave a deep groan. "Tell me that they didn't. They broke it, didn't they? I heard her scream a couple of times. That must have been when that happened." He shoved at the blankets. "I need to see her."

"Not tonight, Dallas." Davy's hand kept him in the bed. "You need to sleep. Tomorrow, we'll get you two together. I understand from Brock that you're heading to their home. At least for now. I agree. It's better that you two are together. It makes it easier to watch out for you."

Dallas nodded, his eyes closing as he slept. Davy watched him for a while before he sat back down. He didn't immediately return to his work, instead thinking through what Dallas had said. To take Dallas down? That had to have included more than an element of surprise. The man must have had either martial arts training or size on his side. Dallas was one of the few people that he knew who could put down just about anyone.

Deri stirred in the early morning hours, a soft moan coming from her. She shifted to her side, pain for a moment stilling her movements. Her eyes opened and like Dallas, she searched her room. She breathed a sigh of relief. *The hospital and I have no idea how I got here. But at least I'm free.* She finally sat up, her hand reaching for the latch on the side rail of the bed and lowering it. Deri swung her feet off the mattress and waited for the room to stop spinning.

She stared down at her hands, seeing the splint on one finger and was afraid. Afraid for her family. Afraid for her friends. And more than that, afraid for Dallas. The men had threatened him the most. She had heard the blows that he had taken. Deri had also heard his struggles to get to her, his shouts for them to leave her alone. It didn't work. She blocked her mind from the pain that she had felt. She would deal with that later.

Rising, Deri headed for the cupboard, hoping that somehow there would be clothes there. *Mom must have been here,* she thought, as she reached for clothes and then dressed rapidly. *Lord, I know You are here. I just don't feel it right now. Please, Lord? Protect my*

Dallas. Don't let them hurt him again. She didn't realize how she had prayed, how important Dallas had become to her.

She hesitantly left her room, wandering the halls, searching for Dallas' room and not finding it. The night nurse watched her for a moment before she approached.

"Deri? Looking for Dallas?" At Deri's nod, she pointed towards the room next to where they were standing. "In there, hon. Go on. It's okay." She wanted as Deri almost ran for the room, hesitating in the doorway before she disappeared.

Deri stood for a moment, blinking in the low light, seeing Davy sound asleep. She smiled. Davy, you are such a friend to us. God is opening you up again. I am glad to see that you are returning to him.

She laid a hand against Dallas' cheek. A prayer for him rose within her. Lord, I don't know where we're going, but You do. Our lives are in Your hand. As I look down the road in the next couple of weeks, we're coming up to Christmas. He'll be with his family, I have no doubt, and I will be with mine. I don't know if I can be happy that day.

Dallas roused, feeling her touch, his hand rising to rest against hers, trapping it against his cheek. His eyes opened and he stared around, looking up at her.

"Deri?" His voice had that early-morning hoarseness, making it even deeper.

"Dallas? You're awake. I didn't mean to awaken you."

"It's okay. What time is it?"

"About five, I think. Are you going home today?"

He smirked. "No."

"You're not? Oh, no! You're hurt that bad." Deri fought the tears that flooded her eyes.

"No, love. I'm going to your place. Your Mom and Dad insisted. Susan and Sean are hidden away right now. The police don't want me at my place." He looked over to where Davy still slept. "Davy made those arrangements."

Chapter 26

Brock watched the younger couple as they moved carefully. It was Saturday morning, three days after they had been rescued. He shook his head. They keep looking at one another and then away. They're falling in love in front of us, don't know what to do, and are afraid to speak with one another. He felt Beth's hand on his back as she leaned against him.

"She's in love, hon."

"That she is. And she is home where we can watch it happen. I don't know what we would have done if she had still been in London."

"We would have managed." Beth sighed. "The house is decorated for Christmas, shopping is done, the baking is done, but I feel as if I am missing something.

"We are. We're in charge of the music for the Christmas Eve service and I haven't had a chance to even think about it. I know I want Deri to sing, if she will, one song. And I would love to have the three sing."

"That would be wonderful. We need that. They have been missed." Beth looked towards the door. "Were we expecting anyone this early?"

"Not that I know of." Brock opened the door to find Davy there. "Davy. Just in time for breakfast."

"I am? Wonderful. I haven't eaten yet. Beth, this is for you." He handed over a beautiful poinsettia plant.

"Thank you, Davy. Now, have a seat. Deri. Dallas. Sit, kids. You need to eat." Beth studied her family as they sat, some laughter but mostly sober looks on their faces. Her eyes rested on Dallas and her heart broke for him. He's hurting in so many ways, Lord,

Davy finally left, leaving a folder for Dallas to look through. The two men had shared a look before Dallas nodded. Is this it, Lord? Have we an answer that will end it all?

Deri had watched the two men before she sighed and headed for the piano, staring at the keyboard before she placed her hands. She could still play, albeit not as well. She had work waiting, she knew, but it would just have to wait. Deri studied the decorations that her mother had placed in the family room and was saddened because it was one more year that she hadn't been able to help. Who knew where she would be next year at this time?

Late that afternoon, Dallas found her as she lay sleeping on the couch. He dropped to the floor in front of the couch, his legs stretched out and crossed as the ankles. Studying the photo Davy had sent him, he sighed. It was the man who had abducted him. Only the man was dead. They would get no answers from him. Davy also said that he had no identification on him. That meant a lot of work. He set the phone down on the floor beside him, becoming lost in thought.

Deri had awakened as he sat down, her eyes on his face. She finally reached out a hand and touched the back of his head, causing him to turn his head towards her.

"Dallas?"

"Deri? I wish this was all over. I want to date you and don't know how to do this."

Deri shrugged even as she sat up. "You never did take me on that date you promised."

Dallas laughed as he raised himself to sit beside her, reaching for her hand, his fingers gentle on the splint as he touched it.

"No, I haven't and I need to. How about lunch tomorrow?"

She stared at him and shook her head. "Not until we heal. Our bruises are brutal, you know."

"I could find some makeup." He laughed as she elbowed him before his arm swung around her and cuddled her close to him.

Deri snuggled down, content, her eyes on the flames flickering in the fireplace, gold, yellow, red and the occasional blue.

"You were troubled just now."

"I was. Davy sent me a photo. It's the man who abducted me. He's dead and they have no identification on him."

"Can I see?" Deri nodded as he searched her face before he handed over his phone. "This man? Oh, I know him. I just don't know his name. He worked security at the studio I used. Oh, no! Did he follow me here?"

"He may have." Dallas sent a quick text off to Davy with that information. "He'll have the detective in London look into that."

The young couple sat, a quiet conversation between long pauses. Beth entered, flicking on the Christmas lights, turning on soft lighting, before she turned. She paused, seeing Dallas with his arm around Deri, her head on his shoulder. She smiled. She remembered what it had been like to be young and in love for the first time.

"Deri?" Beth's voice roused her daughter. "Supper's almost ready. Dad's washing up. Devin won't make it home for supper, he tells me. How be we set up in here and eat? I think we need it."

"Sure, Mom." Deri rose reluctantly, not wanting to leave the security that she had found with Dallas. "Dallas? There are some wooden trays here that we can set up. I'll get the cloths for them. The Christmas ones, Mom?"

"I think so, dear. Now, here's Dad." Beth moved past Brock, a hug given on the way before Deri followed her.

"Dallas? How are you?" Brock studied the younger man, seeing him moving a bit more quickly than he had been.

Dallas shrugged. "Getting there." He paused, biting at his lip, his eyes on the doorway. "Davy was in touch. He sent a photo of my abductor. Deri recognized him as working at the studio she used."

"She did, did she? I was wondering if there was a connection." Brock paused as he took the clothes from Deri and sent her on her way to help her mother. He shot a look after her. "So, tell me. Who are they really after? You? Deri? And you two have never told us what actually happened."

"No, we haven't. We need to talk about it, I guess. No, I know that we need to. We've been avoiding it, I think, just because of the trauma Deri suffered." Dallas watched Deri closely as she set a tray down on one of the tables.

"You're right, Dallas. We do need to talk about it. Dad, we'll eat. Then I need some Dad and Mom prayers."

Chapter 27

Brock finally lifted his head, feeling spent from praying for his daughter and her young man as they now thought of Dallas. Devin had slipped in quietly as they prayed, his tray hitting the table without much of a sound.

"Okay, Deri?" Brock looked at his daughter, curled up on the couch beside Dallas, his arm once more around her. "Care to talk about it?"

Deri shrugged. "I guess. Thanks, Dad. I needed those words. Those reminders. Those verses you quoted." She shared a look with Dallas. "I think that you know what happened to Dallas?"

"No, not really." Devin spoke up, a spoonful of soup held in the air as he did so. "Other than he was abducted from his home."

Dallas spoke quickly, filling them in on what had happened to him.

"Once I was in the building, I was tied to a chair, not able to move. They refused to take the blindfold off. I could hear them speaking with one another but the voices were too low for me to understand. I think there were two and then a third man came in. It was a couple of hours later that I heard Deri." He turned to watch her face, seeing the shuttered look that had descended. *Lord, we need her to talk and not shut down on us.* "Deri?"

She looked up at him and sighed. "I know, Dallas. It's what you tell the victims, isn't it? Sometimes talking about it helps. All right. It's not pretty, Mom and Dad. Devin, I'm sorry. You taught me those martial arts moves and I didn't get a chance to use them." She drew a deep breath.

Deri had finished off the tune that she had been composing and sent it off to Elizabeth, the lyricist that she had been working with. It was one of her better tunes, she thought. I could do this instead of singing myself, she thought. She was on her feet, an eye on the clock. Dallas will be home. We need to talk about some things, Deri thought.

Arriving to find his door ajar, Deri had hesitated about entering, calling for him. She turned to the driveway. His car is here but there is no answer. This is not like him, she thought. She finally pulled out her phone and called Davy. He had been worried about her, she could tell.

With one foot raised, she had been about to enter Dallas' home when Davy's voice stopped her, asking if she was driving and if she was, to head for the detachment and wait for him there. He was on his way to Dallas'.

Frightened, Deri had scurried for her car, stopping abruptly as she saw the man standing beside it. She frantically searched the area, looking for someone, anyone who could help her and finding no one. She turned and ran, hearing the pounding footsteps following her before a heavy body hit her and took her to the ground. Deri had frantically tried to escape, scratching, hitting, and kicking to no avail. The man simply hauled her to her feet and bound her hands behind her. A gag was stuffed in her mouth as she opened it to scream. A blindfold darkened her vision.

Deri felt herself picked up and then quickly dumped into a car, the man sliding in beside her. She heard them talking about her car and felt hands digging into her jacket pocket for her keys. She tried to twist away but the tight hold the man had on her hair prevented that.

She was pulled from the car when it eventually stopped, the grasp back on her hair, and then shoved towards some steps that she stumbled up. Inside, her hands were untied and she was forced to remove her shoes and jacket. Deri found herself shoved down into a chair, her hands bound to the arms.

Dallas had heard the commotion, his head twisting as he searched for the source that he could not see. He groaned. Deri was here. He had prayed that she would not been.

The hours passed slowly. Dallas tried to work his wrists free but was unable to. Deri had tried as well, trying to find a way to free herself. She had cringed away from the man the next day as he had appeared beside her.

"Where is she?" His voice was gruff, coarsened by the tobacco he abused.

"Who? I'm sorry, I don't know who you mean." Deri had been adamant that she had no idea who he was talking about.

The questioning had gone on for a while before Deri had paled.

"I'm going to be sick. I need the facilities." She had repeated herself, her pale face finally moving the man to loosen her bonds and direct her to the washroom. She had rinsed her mouth with cold water when she finished losing the contents of her stomach, the water not really taking away the acid taste.

Shoved back into her chair, Deri had been startled when her left hand had been spread out on the table. A man stood behind her, his hands on her shoulders, holding her down. Another man had stood, his one hand holding her hand still.

The first man kept asking her where the woman was. He gave a coarse laugh when she said she didn't know. Deri's scream of pain had split the air as the heavy object landed on her finger and she heard the snap. Her vision darkened as she heard Dallas' yell of rage and vaguely heard the scuffle behind her. Tears had streamed down her face even as she shook her head. She had no idea who the man was looking for. A second scream of pain came from deep within her as the second bone was broken. Tears flowed as she sobbed.

Dallas struggled to reach her, a fist finding his jaw and knocking him sideways, the force of the blow sending the chair to the floor. His head hit hard, hard enough that he lost consciousness. He didn't hear the begging that Deri was doing, pleading that they didn't hurt him or hurt her again. Whimpers came from her as she bit at her lip at the pain she was put under.

The man had finally stepped back, shaking his head.

"She's not talking." The second man observed.

"No, she's not. Either she doesn't know or she's protecting that woman." The leader looked around. "Okay. Set the bomb. We're out of here. The building will cover them. They'll never be found."

Chapter 28

Brock's face had tightened as Deri had spoken and he heard the soft sobs from Beth as she listened. He didn't need to look at Devin to know what he was feeling. He had always been protective of his sister, that Brock knew, to the point of training her in martial arts at his studio.

Deri had hidden her face against Dallas, not willing to look at her family. His arm had tightened around her. He had known something bad had happened to her when she screamed. It sickened him that they had broken her finger. A thought tickled at his mind before he nodded to himself. He had a good idea who it had been.

Brock rose and came to sit beside Deri, a hand on her head, praying for her. He was heartbroken at what she had suffered. She had gradually been talking to them about what had happened in London. He had been ready to board a plane and travel there to search for the ones responsible for destroying her dreams. Then, he had thought, God was there. He had brought her home at this time. Brock studied Dallas and nodded once more. He's the one that she needs. I can see them falling in love with one another. We would have missed that had she been in London.

"Dallas?" Devin's unspoken question had Dallas looking at him.

"I know, Devin. We need to go back over this but not at this moment. I'll have Deri write it out. Sometimes doing that you get more impressions and can jot them down. She'll remember more and more now that she's opened up." He looked down at her. "I need to find someone for her to speak with."

"Darcie Foster." Deri spoke up, her head raising. "Neasa mentioned her. I want to talk with her if I can."

"Sure. How be we take off tomorrow and head that way? I know her husband, Doug, and also some good friends of hers."

Deri shrugged. "Okay. If you think it's safe."

"Oh, it will be. I can almost guarantee that Breck and Neasa will go with us. He's already been hinting at that."

Deri shrugged. "I don't care." She was on her feet, moving to gather the food trays, heading for the kitchen. The ones left behind could hear her moving around, the sounds of water running, dishes hitting the racks in the dishwasher. They smelt the fresh coffee and tea that she wears making.

Devin was on his feet, heading for the kitchen, meeting Deri as she returned.

"Sis?"

She simply shook her head. "I'm sorry, Devin. Don't ask. I can't talk about it right now." She shoved the tray at him and almost ran for the back door, reaching for her coat, her boots on her feet.

Dallas appeared. "Running again?"

"So it would appear. Who goes after her, you or me?" Devin grinned as Dallas shook his head.

"That would be me. You're too close to her."

"And you're not?" Dallas spun at Devin's words. "We all see it, Dallas. She's depending on you in a way that she doesn't with us. She watches you in a way that I have never seen. She's falling in love. And if you hurt her, you answer to me." Devin turned and walked away, leaving Dallas staring after him.

He reached for his coat, shoving on his boots and then heading outdoors, finding Deri just off the back porch, leaning against the garage. He stopped beside her, his eyes on the night sky. The clear dark blue showed the sparkling stars and the full moon. Dallas simply reached to hug her with one arm.

Deri was startled and then relaxed against him.

"Deri? We don't have to make the trip. We can call."

"We can?"

"We can. We will do what makes you feel the safest." Dallas studied her face. "We still need that date."

"I'm a dangerous person to know."

"And so am I. We really don't know which one this person or persons is after." His cheek leaned against her head. "I was so afraid for you."

"I didn't know that it was you who was there. I knew someone was. I was just so focused on them."

"And the fear drove you to be sick. They used that against you."

"Yes, they did." She looked up at him. "Dallas? Our date?"

"We could go tomorrow or we could pretend that we did and I'm walking you to your door." He grinned at her. Without even thinking it through, he bent and kissed her, his kiss a promise of his love for her.

Chapter 29

Davy watched the next morning as Deri read through the paperwork that he had handed her. He reached for his mug of coffee, sipping it, while thinking back over the early morning. Will had tracked him down about another case, and Davy had responded, then hesitated.

"You wanted to ask something, Davy?" Will watched him carefully.

"I do. This thing with Dallas and Deri. It doesn't make sense. Not at all. Deri shouldn't have been hurt like she was."

"No, she shouldn't. Any thoughts on that?" Will watched him closely, knowing that the skills and instincts he had developed on the street were coming into play.

"I do. There have been rumours around of a man coming into town, looking for Deri. I am still trying to pinpoint who it is but the street is running scared of him. And that doesn't happen. Dallas? I have heard rumours that the same man is after him. Again, no reason was given." Davy was frustrated. "Are they in this together without having met?"

"That's possible. Have we looked at who they know in common, other than the building family and her own family?"

Davy stared at Will and then blinked. "I was starting on that. I had talked to Dallas late last night and gotten a list from him of who he knew here. He also gave names from London. Did you know that he has friends all over?"

Will had grinned. "No, but that does not surprise me, knowing Dallas. He gathers people without realizing that he does so." He paused, a thought coming to him. "You know, so does Deri. This means a lot of contact tracing."

"I know." Davy sounded unhappy and then sighed. "That Emma?"

"Emma? She's sending you reams of information. So is Kataleen." Will continued to grin at the look on Davy's face.

"They are. Who are they?"

"Emma Finlay tracks people. How she finds out information, we don't know. And she has a memory that is scary. Kataleen is married to one of the men in Emma's husband's security team. She has a family tree program that she developed to track contacts and families. They are both the best that I have seen."

"Okay. That makes sense then what I am getting. This Emma has sent stuff I didn't even know I needed."

Will began to laugh at that. "She does. Her mind thinks in a way that most people don't. And if you need security for Dallas or Deri, talk to her husband, Abe. He's already approached me, willing to step in if needed."

"Thanks, Will." Davy gathered up his paperwork and stood. "You know, I can see God in this. He's working on me." Davy walked away, leaving Will staring after him, a brief prayer of thanks raised for that.

Deri finally looked up, bringing Davy back to the present.

"This report, Davy? Why?"

"Because I need you to verify what is in there. I also need to have you prepare a list of any and all your contacts that you had in London. As much as you can."

Deri stared at him and then was on her feet, walking rapidly from the room and then returned with a sheaf of papers in her hands.

"Dallas mentioned this days ago. I have had it done, just not had a chance to give it to you." She sat, shoving the papers at Davy. "Are you thinking that we may have crossed paths other than at that concert?"

"Someone has with the two of you. Why? That I can't answer. Not yet, but I will." He glanced through them. "How are you doing, Deri?"

She shrugged. "As well as I can, I suppose. This bothers me." She held up her hand with the broken finger. "I don't get why. There has to be a reason. They kept asking me about a woman, but that didn't make sense either."

"No, that is strange. We've been trying to work through it." Davy sat back, his eyes on her. "If you had not been found and the finger treated, how would that have affected your work?"

Deri shrugged. "I am sure that I would have managed. I mean, I have a really wide span with my fingers." She stared down at the splint. "If they had continued and broken more, then I don't know."

"Then, why stop?"

"I guess I had lost consciousness. Is that why?"

"Or else they thought that they wouldn't get anything more from you. Do you realize how close it was with the bomb?"

Deri nodded, her face paling even more. "I know." She could barely whisper those words. "Again, why?"

"That we will have to ask them when we find them." Davy gathered his papers. "I am leaving you a copy of that report. Keep it confidential, please. Call or email me if you have any further thoughts." He walked away, leaving her staring after him.

What does he mean, Lord? I don't get this. Deri stared down at the list that she had provided him, her eyes focusing on a name. Is this the one, Lord? I have always felt uncomfortable around him. He watched me too closely. And I saw him watching the others that closely as well. She sent a quick text to Davy and then to Dallas. She had not seen Dallas yet that morning, but she knew that she would. Her face softened as she thought of their conversation the night before. Her finger touched her lips. Dallas had attempted to apologize, but Deri had stopped him with a shake of her head. No, she thought, he is too important to me to let him do that, even though I know why he wanted to. Lord, I have no idea where that's going but You do.

Guard our hearts, dear Lord. Don't let us hurt one another.

Chapter 30

Seated on a bench in a local park, Dallas looked up from where he had been studying the cobblestone path at his feet. He had been asked to meet with someone, and he had not refused. The roughly-dressed man slid down beside him, not looking at him.

"Dallas? You okay?"

"I am. Storm? How about you?"

Storm shrugged. "As well as I can be, I guess. I hear tell that you're having an adventure."

"So it would seem." Dallas shrugged deeper into his jacket, reaching to tighten his scarf. "I worry for Deri."

"I would too. She's in danger, my friend." Storm's eyes searched the area in a way that belied his rough clothing.

"I know. I want to remove it, but I have no idea who is behind it." Dallas didn't look at the man, knowing that was the way they always played it.

"I have a few names that I can give you." Storm reached into his pocket as if searching for coins and laid the paper on the bench between them. "You know them, Dallas. You've had dealings with them." He paused, not sure how to continue.

"And I'm in danger as well. You don't need to say that."

"No, I don't. If you need to hide, you or your Deri, come find me. I'll hide you."

"I am sure that you would." Dallas reached into his pocket for his wallet, pulling it out. "Here. Grab yourself a hot meal and a hot coffee." He handed over a bill, folded over a paper.

"Thanks, man. I can use that." Storm's voice had risen. "It's been a while since I had a hot meal. The shelter's good but they don't let you stay for a long time there."

"No, they can't. We're working on a solution for you. Off with you now."

Dallas watched as he walked away before he shifted on the bench, moving his hand to cover the paper. He let it rest there for a moment before he reached into his pocket for his gloves, hiding the paper in one of them. He rose, heading away, knowing that he was being followed but not really caring that morning. His thought was that if they came after him, he could just maybe capture one of them and end the adventure right then and there.

Heading for his car, Dallas stood for a moment, staring at a store across the street. Running across to it, he entered and then emerged a short time later, tucking a small box into his pocket. He stared around and then his face lit up. Flowers! He could certainly take Deri flowers. He headed for the nearby florist and emerged from it with yellow roses in his hands. He hoped that she would not be offended.

He stood for a moment looking down the street, to where the police detachment was and then shook his head. No today, he thought. I don't need to go there. Davy will find me if he wants to. And I am sure that at some point he will.

Beth stood in the doorway a short time later, a mischievous grin on her face as she watched Dallas approaching her.

"Flowers? Oh, how sweet, Dallas!"

Dallas paused, his face paling as he stared at her.

"I'm sorry, Beth. I should have gotten you some." He stared down at the bouquet.

"It's okay, Dallas. Really. Just having you here is a blessing enough. Come in." She shut the door behind him. "And I suspect that you are looking for Devin. He's not home."

Dallas' eyes narrowed as he continued to stare at her before he grinned, seeing the impish grin on her own face.

"Well, yeah. I could speak with him I guess. But somehow, I don't think he'd want the roses. Nor would Brock."

Beth began to laugh. "She's in the family room, Dallas. You know the way. It's your home, isn't it?" Beth continued to laugh as she turned back to the Christmas baking she was involved in.

Dallas laughed as well before he hung up his jacket, slipped from his shoes, and then picked up the roses. He headed for the family room, hearing Deri's voice and hesitating a moment.

Deri sensed his presence and looked up, a huge smile on her face as she beckoned him to come and join her on the piano bench. He listened as she finished off her conversation and set her phone on the top of the piano. Holding out the roses, he simply waited.

Her face lighting up, Deri stared first at the flowers and then him, watching as he shoved them towards her. She took them, burying her face in them, the fragrance wafting around her. She hugged him and then just sat, not sure what she was to do.

"I guess I did okay?" Dallas' voice was hesitant, not his usual confident tone.

"You did. My favourite colour of a rose." Deri watched him. "Something happened."

"It did. A man from the streets, Storm, approached me. He gave me this." Dallas handed over the piece of paper. "He's sure about this."

Deri took it, her eyes on him before she looked down. "I don't know this person. Should I?" She looked up again when he didn't respond.

"No, you shouldn't. At least I would hope that you wouldn't." Dallas sighed, feeling that he was muddling up everything. "He's someone who is muscle for hire. Storm has confirmed that he is in town and that you and I are targets. He didn't say that in words but he did ask me that if you or I needed to hide that we find him and he would hide us. And he would. He's done that before."

"He has? He would do that without meeting me?"

"He would, love. He would. You're my lady, as everyone seems to think. He would do it for me and then for you."

Chapter 31

The next morning, Dallas stood talking with Brock as he waited for Deri to appear. It was the Sunday before Christmas. This year, he was looking forward to Christmas. He had spoken with both Sean and Susan. They had all agreed that it was best that they not meet at all in person. They had set up a video meeting for Christmas Eve, knowing that Dallas would be with Deri on Christmas Day. Dallas was frustrated. This would have been a wonderful Christmas, he thought, if they hadn't had to be apart.

Turning as he heard footsteps, he paused, drinking in Deri's beauty. Brock watched closely and nodded. Young love, he thought. He remembered that. Lord, protect these two. We're not done with whoever it is that is after them. That scares me.

Deri handed Dallas her jacket and slipped into it, staring down at the hand he had stretched out for her when he had finished before she took it. Brock shook his head as Beth stopped beside him.

"Unsure, aren't they?" Beth hugged her husband. "I remember feeling that."

"As do I. Ready to leave, love?"

"I am." She waited as he locked up and then held the car door for her.

"Just a moment." His phone was vibrating and he looked down at the test. "Jim can't make it this morning. That means I lead." He was speaking of one of the members of his worship team, the man who usually led the singing.

"I guess you do." Beth paused and then shook her head. "Talk to Beck. Maybe he will. We need you on the piano."

"I know."

Dallas watched as Deri twisted in her seat, unable to sit still, before he leaned over, laughter in his voice.

"You're squirmy this morning as my Mom would have said."

She stared at him before she grinned. "I am. I always am the Sunday before Christmas. Ever since I was young." She looked to her other side as Breck poked her.

"You are. Now, behave yourself and sit still." He grinned at her even as Barnabas, Aubrey, and Neasa watched, grins on their own faces.

"And you're not? I know you, cuz. You're just as restless as I am." She laughed as he finally nodded before she jumped as hands rested on her shoulders.

"Okay, you three. Who started it?" Beck's voice held laughter as he studied his son, his niece, and Barnabas.

"They did!" The three friends pointed fingers at one another before they broke out into laughter, bringing smiles to the building family who was seated near them. It was a fact that none of them had seen

Breck and Barnabas like this. Beck shook his head. The three had done that as teens more than once.

"I see. Still blaming each other?" Beck held back his grin even as he held drumsticks in front of Deri's face. "I guess then that I'll just have to have you take my place this morning. I have to lead."

Deri stared at the drumsticks and then twisted to stare at her uncle. "Really? I can?" At his nod, her fist pumped in the air and her feet danced.

Dallas stared at her before he grinned. "You're not enthusiastic enough."

Deri stared at him with narrowed eyes. "You need a bass singer, don't you, Uncle Beck? I know of one who would be glad to volunteer." She smirked at Dallas as he stared at her in shock.

"I can always use a bass singer. In fact, Brock would be more than happy to have him join us." Beck laughed at the expression on Dallas' face even as the ones around waited to see what he would do. He was known to refuse to join any choirs or groups.

Dallas shook his head. She's on fire this morning, isn't she, Lord? I'm glad. I know that we will face things but I love seeing her like this.

"Well then, Beck. I must agree to do this." He smirked in turn at the look on Deri's face before he stood, arm held out for her to walk ahead of him.

Deri was on her feet, hand reaching for Dallas' as she almost dragged him with her. Beck shook his head before he spoke.

"He's good for her."

"He is. And she's bringing him out of his shell." Breck bit at his lip. "I mean. We know him but have never seen him this way."

Davy had stood where he could watch Dallas and Deri. A smile creased his face as he watched them walk, no almost run, he thought, towards the door that led to the basement. They're good for one another. His attention then went to the man who stood just off to the side, intent on the couple, hatred on his face. Davy sighed. This had to happen, didn't it, Lord?

Moving towards the man, Davy's hand on his shoulder kept him in place.

"You seem awful interested in them, my friend."

The man shrugged. "No really."

"No? But you're here, you're watching them, and you were about to walk after them. Right now, I'm intending to find my seat and enjoy the service. I suggest that you sit with me."

"Not happening. I'm not staying." The man turned, staring at the badge that Davy held up, paling.

"I say that you are. Right now, we're going to sit, right here beside Joe. He's another officer." Davy almost shoved him into the pew. "If you try and leave, I'll handcuff you. And when the service is finished, we'll head off downtown and have a little chat, shall we?"

Chapter 32

Early the next morning, Davy stood in Dallas' kitchen, watching the younger man pace. He had appeared just as Dallas was setting his first pot of coffee and gratefully accepted the mug of coffee and offer of breakfast. He had news that he needed to share and he was not certain at all how Dallas would take it.

"You said what?" Dallas spun, his hands gripping the back of a chair with a white-knuckle grasp.

"Yesterday morning in church, I found someone watching you two. I made him sit with myself and Joe and then took him downtown. He didn't want to talk at all at first until I started laying out photos of his work. He is muscle for hire, Dallas."

"Who?" When Davy didn't speak, Dallas spoke again, his voice harsh. "Who was it?"

"Beans Dorsey."

"Beans?" Dallas' brow wrinkled. "I thought that he was dead. That was the scuttlebutt on the street."

"No, he's not dead. That scuttlebutt was wrong. He's here, in our town. He won't say who hired him, only that he was hired to take you and Deri out of the way. Why? That he won't or can't say."

"It's what we expected, isn't it?" Dallas' hands rubbed through his hair and then he stood, hands resting on the sides of his head. "I don't get it, Davy. Why us?"

"That's what we're getting closer to finding out. Apparently, there is a rumour in London that young women musicians were being used to smuggle out stolen jewels and jewellery."

"Deri and her friends?"

Davy nodded. "That's what the thieves seem to want everyone to think. We have confirmation from a couple of the ladies who we spoke with that they had been approached and refused. That is when they began to hear rumours of women who looked enough like them to pass as them at first glance."

"Okay." Dallas moved to pour another mug of coffee, sipping at it without thinking. "So, where is Deri's double?"

"Here in the country somewhere. We think that is who they were looking for when they abducted you two. You were taken likely to make her cooperate."

"We talked about that. It still doesn't make a lot of sense." Dallas spun. "Have you spoken with Deri?"

"She was on the phone bright and early. She would have woken me up if I had been asleep. She received a threatening text that she sent on. She's looking at not using that phone at all except for work."

"Probably a smart move." Dallas watched as Davy rinsed his cup and then dropped it into the dishwasher. "What can I do to help? I feel so helpless right now."

"Your task is to keep yourself and your lady safe." Davy opened his mouth to speak and then just shook his head. "It's coming together, Dallas. It takes time, as you know, and we have other cases that we are working on."

"I know. You can only devote so much to this." Dallas stood in the open door, watching Davy drive away before he reached for his jacket and his keys. He was heading out for the day and knew that he would track Deri down at some point.

He smiled as he remembered how excited that she had been to be able to play the drums. It hadn't been so hard, he decided, to be part of that group, not realizing that it was because Deri was in it that he felt that way. Breck had approached him after the service, pulling him to one side.

"Did Deri say anything to you?"

"About what?" Dallas had frowned at his friend.

"Dad never lets anyone else play his drums. Except for Deri. One day when we were about seven, we had all gathered in the kitchen. Except for Deri. We heard Dad's drums and looked at him. He's sitting there, puzzled before he was on his feet, heading for the room where he had them. He paused at the door, the rest of gathered behind him. Deri was playing them, just as she had seen Dad. We could hardly tell the difference. She looked up, paled, and almost ran to her mother."

"She thought that she was in a lot of trouble?" Dallas could only guess at the emotions that she must have felt.

"She did. Dad crouched down in front of her, holding out his hands, palms up. She finally reached for him and he just hugged her. He had tears in his eyes, thinking that he had scared her. He sat on the floor, Deri on his lap, and talked to her. She apologized for touching them when she wasn't supposed to but she said a voice in her kept telling her that she could play them. And she could. She has had no formal training on them."

Dallas shook his head. "You would never know that. She's been able to do that?"

"All her life. She picks up an instrument and plays it right away. We don't know how she can but it's Deri."

"Thanks for sharing with me, Breck. I appreciate that." Dallas had walked away from his friend, deep in thought, not seeing the woman who was following him.

Chapter 33

Deri threw her phone onto her bed before she covered her face with her hands. The texts were starting to get vicious, she thought. I have no idea who this person is that they are looking for. It's not me. I don't know where the package is that they want. How would I? She pushed the hair back from her face and then grabbed at her phone. Davy needs this, she thought and forwarded it on to him.

Lord, I can't do this. I can't continue like I am, on edge all the time. It's worse than it was in London and that was bad enough. Please, Lord, can we end it and now? She sighed, heading for the stairs. She had work to do and hiding in her bedroom wouldn't get it done.

Hearing the doorbell ring, she detoured to the front door, peering through the window at the couple standing there, just around her own age, she thought, or a little older.

"Can I help you?" Deri held the door open in such a way so that she could slam it shut if she had to.

"You're Deri?" The lady spoke. When Deri nodded, her smile grew. "I knew it was. I just knew it. I'm Elizabeth and this is my Nathaniel. We've been working together on songs. I am Lyrics by Whizz."

"Elizabeth? Oh, how wonderful! Come on in. And your husband? Here, let me have your coats." Deri quickly directed them to the family room. "You've travelled. Coffee, tea?"

"Coffee sounds wonderful, Deri." Nathaniel spoke up. "Let me help you." He followed her through to the kitchen, watching as she prepared the tray before he reached for it. "You have a lovely home."

"Dad and Mom have remodelled over the years to get it to this point. When I was growing up, it felt like we were always torn apart." She thanked him before she sat in her favourite chair, her eyes on Elizabeth.

"Elizabeth?" Deri finally got up the courage. "You're here. I don't understand."

"It's like this." Elizabeth shared a look with Nathaniel who had been watching Deri closely. "Emma sent me. Nathaniel is one of the men on Abe's security team. Abe has been concerned about what Dallas is talking to him about. He wanted us to come by and see what we can do." Elizabeth grinned. "Besides, I wanted to meet in person with the lady I've been working with and put a face to the voice."

Deri smiled. "Thank you for that." She turned to Nathaniel. "Security?"

"That's right. We used to go in and bring people out of situations. Now, we mostly do training."

"And you would be on the team?"

He continued to grin. "The sniper. And I have never had to do that."

"You haven't? Isn't that unusual?"

Nathaniel nodded. "It is." He looked around as he heard the door in the kitchen open and close. "If you don't mind my asking, were you expecting someone?"

Deri shrugged. "Mom. Devin, my brother. Dad. Breck or Neasa or Aubrey." She felt the hands on her shoulders. "Or some pest named Dallas."

"Pest, am I?" Dallas dropped a kiss on her cheek before he sat on the floor at her feet. "Nathaniel? You're here. And with Elizabeth."

"We are. I wanted to meet Deri. I have some more lyrics for her that I would love to have her take a look at. That last song we did? The one about returning to God? The artist loved it. She wants as many as we can get to her. She really doesn't care about the theme, as long as they honour God and how He protects us."

"And He does that." Deri's face glowed. "Oh, this is so wonderful. And we really are not that far apart, are we?"

"No." Nathaniel shared a look with Dallas who rose and headed for the kitchen.

"It's almost lunchtime, Deri. I'll work on something for us."

"Are you sure?" She peeked around the chair at him, finding him watching her.

"I am. And you are going to share what happened this morning."

Deri sighed. "I knew you would say that. Take this. Look at the last text. I've already sent it on to

Davy." Her hand went up and over her shoulder as he reached for her phone. "It's getting bad, Dallas."

"I'm sure it is. Nathaniel here will likely have a laundry list of suggestions for us."

"A laundry list?" Nathaniel laughed. "I could do. All eight of us got together as well as some friends. Having gone through so much ourselves, we want to keep you two safe."

Deri's eyes shot to Elizabeth, who nodded. "We did. It wasn't nice. Abe and our police chief, good friends of mine, by the way, decided that I needed a boyfriend. They nominated Nathaniel without asking him. Long story short? We came through with some bumps and bruises but in love and now married."

"Is that how it's supposed to be? I mean, I don't think we're supposed to be in danger to find our life mates."

"No, we're not. But sometimes that is how God works it. He also uses times like these to bring us closer to Him."

"And that He does." Deri looked up, hope on her face. "She really liked that song?"

"She did, Deri. She did. I spoke with her on the way over. If I have your permission, I will give her your phone number and she can call you."

"Oh, please! You don't know how much I need this. I mean, I have my songs that are out there but to do this? For someone well known? It's a God moment, don't you think?"

Chapter 34

Dallas turned from the French doors in the family room later that afternoon, finding Deri hesitating in the living room. He walked towards her just as she entered the doorway, his arms around her.

"Deri?"

"Dallas? When will this be over? I am so tired of living like this. It went on for close to a year in London before I fled."

"I know, love. I know." He hugged her tight, his head resting against hers before he looked up and smiled. Beth?

"I want it over." Deri's face was upturned to his just as he kissed her. She shoved at him. "Dallas? What?" Her voice was stilled with another kiss. Every time she opened her mouth, he kissed her.

Brock and Beth were working together on supper in the kitchen, hearing Deri's voice stilled every few moments. He reached over to kiss Beth.

"I think our daughter is being kissed, love."

"I think so." She leaned against him for a while. "I'm glad she's home but I wish it had been under different circumstances."

They both looked around as Devin entered, barely able to contain his mirth.

"Devin?" Beth frowned at him.

"It's okay, Mom. Deri doesn't realize that she's standing right under the mistletoe."

"She doesn't? Oh, I meant to warn her." Beth dried her hands, intent on heading that way when Brock's hand stopped her. "Brock?"

"Let it be. He'll tell her. Eventually." He shared a grin with his son. "Off to find Kara?"

"I am, Dad. We're having dinner with her folks tonight. We may stop by later."

"That's good. Enjoy yourself."

Dallas finally stepped back from the doorway, pulling Deri with him. Her face was rosy as she looked up.

"Your Mom hung mistletoe." He smiled as she looked at him horrified for a moment.

"She did? Oh, no! I forgot. I'm not usually here for Christmas. She's hung it there for years." Her eyes narrowed as she stared at him. "And you took advantage of that."

"I did and I am sorry. I shouldn't have."

"Really? You kiss me and then apologize? Make up your mind, buster." She went willingly into his hug.

"You're not mad." Dallas stood for a moment just holding her. "We need to talk about that text message."

"And about what Nathaniel gave us." Deri sighed. "He seems to think that it will get much worse."

"And it will. I'm sorry, love. I wish I could stop it now but we have no idea who is behind it all. I talked with Davy earlier today. He has word that the woman who looks so much like you. That group were jewel smugglers. Some of your friends have confirmed that they were approached and refused."

"I wasn't. That's makes this so bizarre." Deri moved away, heading for the kitchen. "We will talk, Dallas, but for now can we set it aside?"

Dallas reached to stop her, his hand finding her left hand, his finger rubbing at her ring finger. Deri stared at their hands and then up at him, a puzzled look on her face.

"Dallas?" Her voice was barely audible, uncertainty in it.

"It's okay, love. It's okay." He looked down at her, a look in his eyes that had her face softening and a soft glow coming to it. "We need to talk about us. I am in love with you, Deri. And that scares me."

"You are? Oh!" Deri reached to hug him. "Thank you, Dallas. I thought I was in love with someone who wouldn't return my love."

"You were? And you are?" Dallas kissed her again. "We'll talk, love. We'll really talk but for now, I think your parents are likely wondering where we are."

Deri hugged him again before she stood back, a frown passing over her face. "Okay. We'll eat. Then Mom and Dad will want to talk about the Christmas Eve service. Dad's in charge of the music."

"Is he? Does that mean you sing?" Dallas swung an arm around her as they turned for the hallway.

"I think so. I know he wants Barnabas, Breck and I to sing."

"I would enjoy that. I am sure the church family would as well."

Deri shrugged. "I guess. I'm just not into that all that much this year."

"No, given what you are going through, you wouldn't be."

Chapter 35

Christmas Eve found the group gathering with their church family. Deri nestled down next to Dallas, her eyes on the people gathering, having missed that for so many years. She sighed. She was home but still felt unsettled. Going through what she was meant that she couldn't really get back into life in her town. She was too afraid to get close to anyone in case they were hurt.

Aubrey was seated beside her and reached for her hand.

"I hear that you three are singing tonight." She watched her friend closely.

"We are." Deri sighed again. "I know we should but I am just so torn by it all."

"You will be until whoever it is that is chasing you is found. I can understand that feeling." She shared a look with Dallas. "He'll want to protect you in any way that he can."

"I know." Deri's face softened as she turned to Dallas. "He tries, you know."

"I do, do I?" Dallas grinned at her before he looked past the ladies to Breck, who was listening closely. "For tonight, we set it aside and enjoy this time. Tomorrow, we enjoy ourselves with our families. And then the next day, we can get back to work solving this. I would imagine the building fellows have been at work. Breck?"

"That they have been, Dallas. Only this time, they can't figure it out. Blair tells me that there are too many strings."

"Then, we start pulling strings and finding out which ones we can eliminate." Dallas turned to the front. "Aren't you supposed to be up there?"

Deri shook her head. "I told Dad that if I was singing in the trio, I didn't want to be involved. He was fine with that."

Late that night, Dallas paced his home office. He was restless but exhausted. He knew that he should retire but just couldn't bring himself to.

Heading for the kitchen to refill his coffee mug, Dallas paused as he heard a tap at his back door. Flicking off the lights, he headed that way, standing to the side as he peeked out.

"Dallas? It's Storm. Let me in. Please?"

Dallas cracked open the door enough that Storm could enter, closing and locking it after him. He simply pointed to his office and then fixed a tray with a mug of coffee and food for Storm.

He watched Storm for a moment before he nodded. He's not here out of the blue, is he, Lord? Not on Christmas Eve. He should be with his family, not here.

"Storm?" Dallas sank down into his desk chair, reaching for a pen and pad of paper.

"Thanks, Dallas. This hits the spot. I didn't get a chance to grab my supper before the diner closed." Storm bit into the sandwich and chewed and then swallowed. "Is your lady okay?"

"She was when I left her. Why?"

"Because you were watched going to your church, while there, and then while at her parents'. They are getting desperate, Dallas. Word on the street is that an attempt will be made to grab her over the next couple of days."

Dallas slid his eyes shut even as he groaned. "That's what we are afraid of. Any idea on who?"

"Not really and that's strange. Whoever it is has hidden in shell companies, Dallas. I know Davy has had someone working on that." Storm finally rose, heading for the door, before he paused. "Stay safe, Dallas. As I said, you need any help or your lady does, come find me. I'll be hanging close to her."

"Thank you, Storm. I appreciate it. You stay safe as well."

Chapter 36

Late Christmas afternoon, Dallas slumped down in the corner of the couch, Brock in his easy chair nearby. It had been a draining day emotionally, he thought. This is when I miss my parents and sister. Not having Susan and Sean around doesn't help. His chin rested on his upraised fist. Dallas was oblivious to the regard that Brock had him under.

"Dallas?" Brock's voice brought his attention to the older man. "Do we need to have a talk, you and I?"

Dallas studied him, seeing the concern but interest on his friend's face. "About what?" He was not about to jump into it, he thought. He had a good idea what Brock was after.

"About you. About my baby girl. About the two of you?" Brock watched him closely, a slow smile spreading across his face. He saw the calm face that Dallas presented but saw the mischief lurking in his eyes. "Not talking, are you? I can see that. Just wanted to know if you do indeed love my baby girl."

"That is a conversation that I have with Deri first. Then, just maybe we'll talk. Dad." Dallas bit back his grin as Brock nodded and then did a double-take, his eyes narrowing as he stared at Dallas.

"Dad, is it? Well then, son, welcome to the family. I would gather by that you two have talked. I, no, Beth and I could not ask for someone better suited to our girl." Brock looked around as he heard the ladies heading their way. "And if you need to talk, come find me."

"I will, thanks, Brock." Dallas rose to take the tray from Beth, watching as they helped themselves to their mugs of tea or coffee and the plate of iced fruit cake or cookies or squares before he took his own and sat back down beside Deri, who crowded close to him.

"Where does the investigation stand, Dallas?" Beth had her eyes on Brock, a narrowed look to them.

"That I don't know. Breck said there are too many strings. I suggested that we need to start pulling some."

"What you're saying is that it is as tangled as those lights I had to untangle to put on the tree?" Brock nodded that way. "Okay. I don't work tomorrow. How be we set up in my office here and get to work? Would that help?"

"I think it would, Dad." Deri stared at her father. "You haven't said much."

"No, I haven't. Not because I haven't wanted to but because I have no idea what you have in information or thoughts."

"You're right, Dad. We haven't shared. Not because we haven't wanted to. I just didn't think of it." Deri blinked rapidly. "So, tomorrow, we gather what we have. It's not pretty, Dad, Mom."

"We didn't suspect that it would be, love." Beth sipped at her tea. "Let's set it aside for now and just enjoy some time together. It's been such a rush up until now. Devin and Kara are away now at her parents'. They may be back here later, but he wasn't sure."

"I don't think they will, Mom. I saw Devin tucking a small box into his jacket pocket. I suspect he's ready to ask."

"He is." Brock studied the younger couple, seeing Dallas hiding a smile. "Anything that you two want to share?"

"Such as?" Deri just laughed at her father as he shrugged, hands in the air. "Don't worry, Dad. We'll tell you when we think that you can handle the news."

"I see. And you don't think that I can?" Brock laughed at his daughter before he sobered. He reached for his Bible. "Before we go any further, I know that we read the Christmas story this morning. I would like to go back and read some of the prophecies that foretold Jesus' birth."

"That would be nice, Brock. Dad used to do that Christmas Eve." Dallas settled back, his arm around Deri.

Chapter 37

Beth stopped at her daughter's bedroom door the next morning and watched for a moment as Deri sorted papers on her bed. She finally approached her, an arm around her and an audible prayer sounding in Deri's ear.

"Deri?"

"Mom?" Deri looked at her mother. "Is something wrong?"

"No. I'm just worried about you." She began to smile. "Your father said he tried prying last night but Dallas didn't bite."

Deri began to laugh. "That's what Dallas said. He won't get any information from Dallas unless he chooses to let him."

"I know." Beth dropped a kiss on her daughter's face. "Dallas is the one who completes you, makes your heart whole. We all see that. I have no idea where you stand and I won't ask. You'll talk to us when you're ready."

"We will, Mom. We have talked but this, whatever this is, keeps getting in our way. It didn't spoil our Christmas Day but it might yet spoil the season."

"Nothing will spoil the reason, love. Nothing. We are praying for you both. Now, I hear your young man's voice downstairs. Your father told him that he might as well move in, he's here that much."

"He didn't!" Deri began to laugh. "Dad is something else."

"That he is. Come down when you're ready." Beth turned to walk away.

"Mom?" Beth turned at the tone in her daughter's voice, suddenly afraid. "You and Dad just had a small wedding, didn't you? Do you regret that?"

"Not at all. It is what we wanted. The people who mattered were there." Beth hugged her daughter. "And if you're asking, have the size of wedding that you want. Small or large, that is your decision. Yours and Dallas'. Although I suspect that his friends will want to be there. And then there are the officers that he worked with."

Deri chewed at her lip before she gathered up her papers. "That's the thing, Mom. How would we ever narrow it down?"

"Have his friends and fellow officers for the wedding, have a smaller reception, and then an open house later for his fellow officers."

"Thank you, Mom." Deri reached to hug her mother before she danced away. "You just solved a question that we both had."

Beth stared after her, praying hard for her daughter. Lord, I have no idea what this was all about, but You do. Please, Lord, protect them? Let their plans come to fruition.

Brock looked up from his computer a few hours later, frustrated. He looked around and then headed for the basement, returning with a roll of newsprint. Dallas' hands were there to help.

"Where do you want this, Brock?"

"On that wall. Here's some painter's tape to attach it." Brock was sorting through markers, finding the ones that he wanted. "Here. I have a selection of different colours. How would you work this, Dallas?"

"How?" Dallas stared at the paper. "By first listing what we know. The people involved. The confirmed items. And we do have confirmed items, even though Davy can't share a lot with us. Breck was by earlier today and left a sheaf of papers from the fellows." He pointed to the coffee table. "That's what that is."

An hour later, Dallas stepped back and nodded. Brock's idea of colour-coordinating the information helped, he thought. He didn't remember anyone else doing that.

"Brock? Why the colours?"

Brock looked up. "From my work. You know that I am a painter. Some people want coordination with their colours. Others don't. It just made sense to coordinate the information that way."

"I agree." Deri moved close to Dallas, his arm around her. "I can see it plainer that way. It's what you've always done, Dad. It's how I think and I haven't done that with this."

"So, what can we then eliminate?" Beth moved to her daughter's side. "We need another piece of paper or your word processor program, Brock."

"We need Devin with his computer skills. He could set up a database for us and we could work from there." Brock looked around. "Devin and Kara! Just who we needed to see."

"And good afternoon to you too, Dad. What are we up to?" Devin and his girlfriend greeted the others.

"Dad wants to set up a database of some kind, transfer this information and then sort it." Deri had put it concisely what Brock had wanted.

"Is that all? Sure. Kara's the programmer. She can help that way."

"I sure can. Brock?"

"Here you go, love. Sit right down here. This is what I am thinking." Brock went into detail about what he was thinking.

Listening to Kara and Brock discuss his ideas, Dallas shook his head. They didn't work that way at the police but this wasn't the police. He could bring his experience in but he would wait for that. They would ask, he felt, if they wanted his advice.

Deri pulled him away with her, heading for the kitchen, an eye on the clock.

"We have time to make pizzas for supper. We need something different for tonight."

"That we do." Dallas paused her steps in the kitchen and bent to kiss her.

———

Deri felt him move away and opened her eyes, to find him on his knee in front of her, her hand in his. Her free hand went to her mouth.

"Deri, no matter what happens, you are the love of my life. I never thought that I would find her, but I did. Will you marry me, be my companion through the years?" He held up a beautiful ruby ring.

She nodded, unable to speak, tears blinding her as he slipped the ring on her finger and then rose to gather her close. Deri finally had a chance to study her ring and was puzzled.

"A ruby?"

Dallas nodded. "My Proverbs 31 lady."

They spoke for a few more moments before Deri pulled out the fixings for their supper.

"We can't hide my finger, you know?"

"No, we can't but that's okay, isn't it?"

Deri stared at her fingers, one with a splint and one with a ring. "This is odd, you know. Thank you, sweetheart." She reached to return his kiss.

Chapter 38

Dallas turned the next morning as he heard his name called. Will was walking towards him from the other side of the street.

"Time for a coffee, Dallas?"

Dallas grinned. "I do but do you?"

Will grinned in response. "I do. We need to have a chat, Dallas."

"We do, don't we?" Dallas slid into the booth in the nearby cafe. "First, let's order and then we talk."

"We do, and we pray as well. I have missed those times with you." Will looked up with a word of thanks as the waitress set down their coffees.

"I haven't talked to Davy if that's your concern. He has told me what he can."

"I know, Dallas. That's not an issue. I had a long chat with Brock last night."

"You did? That doesn't surprise me. I guess he told you what we were up to?"

"He did and I agree with him that you needed to. Deri needs that visual to help her cope." Will watched Dallas closely. "He also had some other news."

"He did, did he?" Dallas grinned. "We're engaged." He held up a hand. "I know that we haven't known each other long but we love each other, Will."

"I know. I saw that on Christmas Eve. You're good for her, Dallas. And she's bringing out your fun side, I hear tell."

Dallas grinned again before he sobered. "But you wanted to talk." He bit into his piece of toast, watching Will closely.

"I do. It's almost the end of the year, Dallas. You put in your resignation effective on the 31st. I can accept that but you will be missed. You have an insight into people and situations that few have."

Dallas shrugged. "It's just the way my brain works, I guess. I will miss the people I worked with, the people that I helped, but not the burden."

"Burden? That's a good way to put it. I spoke with John and Bruce earlier. Everything that you need is in order to start your new work on the second." Will paused, his eyes on the pedestrians outside, zeroing in on one particular man. "You will do well in your new duties. That I know already. You have a giving heart and a compassion that I don't often see in our officers."

"Thanks, Will. I needed that today." Dallas' eyes were on the crumbs that he was moving around the table with his finger. "Did Brock talk much to you about what we had discovered?"

"He did. It concerns me, Dallas, let me tell you that. This is when it gets hard, as you know. Kara does good work."

"She does. She's known for that in our community of law."

"I know that you and Deri and her family will work with us. Don't go running out there on your own." Will finally sat back. "Let me pray with you, Dallas. One last time as one of my officers."

Dallas blinked, his emotions almost getting the best of him before he nodded. "I would like that, Will. I will miss those times."

Dallas stood an hour later, staring at his vehicle. Something was definitely off about it. He sighed and pulled out his phone, calling for assistance.

The bomb squad leader walked towards him later, pulling off his helmet.

"Dallas? What are you mixed up in? First that house and now this?"

"I have no idea. I just felt something off about this. What did you find?"

"A bomb that would have gone off when you hit the key fob." His hand was out for Dallas' keys. "Let me see them." He studied them. "Here." He pointed to the lock. "See this? You would have been close enough to be hurt or killed if you had hit this."

Dallas paled. "I would have? That's what they tried with the building, wasn't it? So who wants me dead? Or is it to get to Deri?" He paced before a hand on his arm stopped him. "Will? You're here?"

"I am. I was in a meeting when the call came in. Dallas?"

Dallas shrugged. "I don't know, Will. I just don't know." He spun to face him, a sudden thought coming to his mind. "We never found Deri's car, did we?"

"No, we didn't." Will pulled out his phone at the insistent chiming and moved away to take the call. He spun, shock on his face as he sought to find Dallas. He moved back in, a hand on Dallas' arm, pulling him away from his fellow officers. "Dallas? I need you to come with me."

"Will?" Dallas clicked his seatbelt closed even as Will took off, sirens blaring and lights flashing. He watched as Will pulled to a stop near the outskirts of town. "Why here?"

"Stay put for a moment. In the car." Will emphasized that. "Right now? Storm got word to us that someone has taken out a hit on you. He's working on getting more information. I don't want you in the open. Not until I come back." Will was out of his car and moving towards where the activity was.

As the men and women moved around, Dallas glanced that way and then stared hard. His head went back even as his eyes closed. A groan pulled from deep within him. That was Deri's car. The one that they had not been able to find. Well, Lord, what surprises do we have now? He watched as the medical examiner moved in, his hand reaching for the door handle before he pulled it back. No, he thought, I had promised Will.

Will approached and motioned him to come with him.

"Will?" Dallas was confused, not something that usually happened to him.

"It's Deri's car, Dallas. It gave us all a start. There is a female inside dead."

"Dead?" He paled and then staggered. "Not Deri!"

"No, it's not. It's the female that looked like her." Will watched as Dallas processed the information.

"She's been found? Now what?" Dallas stared down at the face of the female before the body bag was closed. He looked up, relief coursing through him that it wasn't his beloved Deri, but wishing that the woman was still alive so that they could speak with her. "Is she the one that they were looking for when they hurt Deri?"

Chapter 39

Deri turned later that morning as Dallas' arms simply swept her close to him. She clung to him, feeling the tremors running through his body. She finally shoved at him, moving back to watch him, knowing something had happened.

"Dallas?"

"Deri! You have no idea what I just went through. I am so glad that you are here and safe." He pulled her back against him, his eyes on Brock as he stood frowning at him. Beth had appeared as well as had Devin.

"Dallas?" Brock's voice finally broke through the silence. "Something has happened."

"It has. Deri's car was found this morning on the outskirts of town." He paused, swallowing hard.

"They found it? Can I go get it?" Deri's voice sounded loud in his ears for a moment. She frowned as he shook his head. "Why not?"

"Because it's a crime scene, love. It wasn't empty when they found it." Dallas kept his eyes on his beloved Deri. "The woman who looked like you? She was in it."

Deri paled as she swayed for a moment, Dallas' arms keeping her on her feet. "Dead? Oh, no! No, I don't want that car back."

174

"What can you tell us, Dallas? And I am gathering Will has allowed you to talk to Deri." Brock moved away to lean against the counter.

"He did. I don't know much. They were just starting the investigation. And that's not all. Will and I had a meal earlier this morning. I went back to my car. God stopped me in my tracks. I could not take another step towards it. There was a bomb set to go off once I hit the lock on the key fob."

Deri paled and then hugged Dallas tighter.

"Dallas? They're after you?"

"Someone is. That's what Storm has found out." Dallas shared a look with both Brock and Devin. "I will be careful. I promise you that, love."

"What plans do we make?" Devin pulled out the sandwiches that had been made. "It's lunchtime. We eat. Then we pray. Then we plan."

Raising his head after their time of prayer, Dallas felt refreshed but still worried. His eyes found Deri as she moved around the kitchen with her mother, not comfortable that she would be safe.

"How bad, Dallas?" Devin kept his voice low.

"Bad enough. There's a hit out on me, Storm says. Whether it's related to this or something else, we don't know yet."

"Dallas, your parents and sister? Did they ever find out who did it?" Beth stood beside him, her arm around the shoulders of the man she considered her second son.

Dallas nodded. "I got word about a month ago that they finally had them. After all this time." He looked down at the table. "It was a friend of Dad's. He hasn't talked as to why but the investigators say that robbery was likely the reason. Apparently, my parents and sister walked in on him robbing the house. He shot them and then disappeared without taking anything."

Chapter 40

New Year's Eve day found Dallas in his office at the police detachment, staring around at the office that he had occupied for what seemed so many years. It wasn't really, he thought. He had risen rapidly through the ranks, he knew, more rapidly than was wont. He had nothing left there in the office, having cleared it out before he went on leave.

Staring down at the badge and police-issue weapon, Dallas wondered for a moment if he had made the right choice. He nodded. He had prayed it through. His friends had prayed for him, not knowing what the request was. When Bruce had approached him about taking on a new role with the Foundation, that of an investigator in a new department that they were looking at, he had nodded, asked to have time to pray about it, and then felt God's peace in his heart as he had made his decision.

He walked rapidly towards his supervisor's office, knocking and then entering. His supervisor was waiting. A few quiet words and Dallas turned over his badge and weapon, turning at last to leave the place where he had spent so many hours.

Walking the streets of the downtown, at a loss for a moment, Dallas paused before a store. No, he thought. I don't need any books, do I? He walked on, nodding and speaking to friends and acquaintances. Breck watched him walking towards him.

"Dallas?"

Dallas looked up, startled. "Breck?"

"I'm here. I knew you would be down here. Time for a coffee?"

Dallas shrugged. "All the time in the world. How about you?"

"I do."

Breck watched his friend walk away later that morning. They had talked, had prayed but Breck was still uneasy. Something is about to happen, isn't it, Lord? Protect him. Protect Deri.

Deri walked into Dallas' hug, knowing how difficult it had been. Her prayer for him whispered in his ear before she stepped back.

"Dallas?"

He shrugged before he smiled at her. "I'm okay. Now, where are we in our investigation?"

"I have no idea. People just moved in and took over on me."

"They did? Who?" He looked past her towards the hallway.

"Abe and Emma and Nathaniel and Elizabeth were here. They couldn't stay for long, they said. It was long enough for Abe and Nathaniel to look over what we had done and make some suggestions. Emma had a pile of material for us, all sorted and everything."

"Wonderful. Can we get started on it?" He looked down at her as she shook her head.

"Not today. Today, we set it aside. Neasa called. They're having a gathering at the building and want us there, seeing as you now work for the Foundation."

"Not until the second, but sure. Do you want to?" Dallas watched her closely, trying to assess how his new position would affect her.

Deri shrugged. "We can if you like. I mean, they are all friends."

"You don't have any other plans?"

She shook her head. "Not for today. Tomorrow, we are to go to Uncle Beck's, if you want to."

"Sure. Breck mentioned that this morning when we had coffee."

"Oh. But for now, we need to make some other plans." She pointed towards the family room. "I'll grab our hot drinks."

Dallas waited, taking the tray from her and then following her to the room that they had claimed as theirs.

"We'll need to get you a piano, love."

"We will. All in good time. For now, we have a mystery to solve." She nestled down beside him, content she thought for the first time in a long time. "That woman in my car? Any more news?"

"None. That's not surprising."

Chapter 41

The next morning, Beth frowned as she paused at Deri's door. It was wide open and the bed seemed to be the very same as she had left it the morning before. She searched the house, not finding her daughter. Text messages and phone calls went unanswered. Beth turned as Brock entered from outside, his hat and coat on the rack before his boots hit the tray.

Brock turned, finding Beth standing in the middle of the kitchen, her hand on her face, fear on it as well.

"Beth?" Brock's hands were on her arms.

"Deri. She's not in the house. And her bed has not been slept in."

"What? And you called?"

"I did. I was just about to call Dallas."

Brock did that, frustrated that he got no answer. He reached for his coat and boots.

"I'll head that way. You call Breck. They were all together last night."

Beth turned as Devin entered, fear on her face. He had not been home that night, spending it with Kara and her family.

"Devin? Have you spoken with Deri today?"

Devin looked around at his mother, seeing the fear on her face. "No, I haven't. I sent a text message earlier but she didn't answer. I didn't think much of it."

"She's not home. Dad has gone to find Dallas if he can."

"He has? Let me try again."

Beth's hand stopped him. "She's not replying, Devin, no matter what we try."

Devin grew stern. "Breck?"

"I spoke with him. They left about one, he said, planning on Dallas dropping Deri off and then heading home."

Devin's phone was back out and Beth heard him speaking with the authorities. It wouldn't get shuffled under the pile, she hoped but knowing that as adults, it just might.

"I spoke with Davy. He's on his way with a team. He expected something like this, he said."

Davy stared at the tech who was pointing to the ground.

"You found something?"

"I did. A lot of footprints. A female and at least three male. I would suspect Dallas and Deri." The tech turned. "Right here by the driveway. Once they're back on the pavement, I can't follow them."

"Get me what you can. I don't have to tell you that Dallas has a hit out on him."

"He does?" The tech paled. Dallas had been a favourite with the techs, working with them as much as he could and they would allow to find evidence. "On it, Davy. I'll call with what news I have."

Brock stood on the sidewalk watching closely before Davy moved his way.

"I don't like the looks of that conversation."

"Nor did I. It appears that they arrived here and then were taken from here. You didn't hear anything?"

Brock shook his head. "Once I'm asleep, I don't hear much. Beth might have."

"I'll need to speak with you and Devin. Where were they last night?"

"At the Foundation building. At their get-together, seeing as Dallas will be working there."

Davy sighed. "Okay. I'll have officers head that way and talk to them all. This was supposed to stop with Barnabas."

"Was it? Well, it certainly doesn't seem to have." Brock nodded towards the house. "Are you free to come and speak with Beth?"

"I'll be in shortly, Brock." Davy watched as Brock moved away, shaking his head. Where are you two? This was not supposed to happen, now was it?

———

Chapter 42

Two days passed without any word from the couple or about them. Davy worked almost non-stop around the clock before Will stepped in and sent him home, telling him that he needed to rest. Beth and Brock roamed the house, Devin heading out every day with Kara at his side, searching. Breck and Beck had been around. Bonnie almost lived in Brock's home, making meals, cleaning, praying, and just being there.

The building men had taken a look at each other and then headed for the conference room, pulling up the programs that they had used to solve the mysteries of the fourteen of them. It was to no avail. Not even Emma had been able to help. It was as if they had disappeared off the face of the earth.

Brock paced his home office. He was due out the next day to start a painting job but just didn't have the heart to do it. He sighed as he glanced towards the doorway, knowing that Beth was curled up in the family room, not wanting to move.

Beth looked up as Neasa handed her a cup of tea and then sat beside her.

"Aunt Beth? What can I do for you?" Neasa grasped the shaking hand that Beth extended to her.

"I don't know, Neasa. I really don't. It's not like they would have just up and left. One of them would have let us know, given what's been going on. They would have at least responded to a text message." Beth wiped at the tears trickling from her eyes.

Breck walked in at that point followed by Barnabas and Bruce. They exchanged a look with Neasa before Bruce turned and walked away, heading for Brock's office.

"Brock?" Bruce sat beside the man, prayers raising for him.

"Bruce? Where's my baby girl?" He was devastated and it showed on his face and in the uneasy movements that he was making.

"We'll find her. I promise you that, Bruce. Now, about tomorrow? You're back at work?"

"I am. I have no choice. Only, I have no idea how I am going to do that."

"I spoke with Will. He has an officer that he's sending with you. He does painting on the side. I've seen his work. He's good."

"Will would do that?"

"He would. He's putting an officer here in the house as well with Beth. Devin has refused one."

"He would." Brock drew a deep shaky breath. "We'll do what we can. What I don't understand? We have had no calls for ransom or anything."

"We know. They're not after that, Brock. They're after whatever it is that they think Deri has."

"And she has nothing. Not that she is aware of." Brock looked up. "Would she be offended, do you think, if we looked through her things?"

"Davy will want to. He's on his way in."

Brock nodded before he arose and headed for Beth.

"Beth? Davy's on his way over. He'll want to look through Deri's things."

"I know, Brock. I have pulled everything out and put it on her bed. Other than her laptop and I can't access that."

"That's okay. He'll look through what you have put out."

Davy stood an hour later. "I don't see anything here. Her laptop?"

"She has it set up as password protected. I have no idea what the password would be." Beth folded her arms around herself.

"That's okay. If I need to, I'll get a warrant and take it to one of our techs. She's good at breaking the password."

Devin stood in the doorway. "Her laptop? I can access it but I gather you would need a warrant to do that."

"Legally, I would. And I won't ask you to do that." Davy was at a loss. They had been searching, officers on their own time, and had no idea where the two were."

Devin followed him outside, standing with his hands jammed into his jeans pockets.

"Davy? What are your thoughts?"

Davy shrugged, his eyes on the horizon. "To tell you the truth, Devin? There are just so many possibilities. I would suspect Dallas was taken, either because he refused to leave her or to use it as leverage against her. Deri? We're still tracking down all the threads from London. Although that seems to be a dead-end where she is concerned. She is correct in that she was never asked to do anything for anyone."

"What does that leave us?"

"Something from here." Davy turned to Devin, hope in his eyes. "Did anything happen when she was still home or at home at any time that you can think of?"

Devin shrugged in his turn. "She never said. Not that I can remember. She might have to Breck or Barnabas." Devin suddenly paled. "I remember. It was her last year at university. She had been away on a tour with the school and came home. She was really quiet, not saying much. I asked her what was wrong. She had looked at me and said that she had seen something in town that bothered her but she wasn't quite sure what to make of it. She really didn't say much more than that, no matter how much I tried to get her to. That's when I made her start self-defence classes."

"You did? Good. Now, what would she have seen?"

"That she really didn't say. One day, just before she moved to London, she was looking at something on Dad's bookshelf and I heard her muttering. Something about a man in town who wasn't what he seemed. I looked at what she had been looking at. It was a statue, I think or a book." Devin was running for the stairs, Davy at his heels.

Brock and Bruce looked up as the two men ran into the room and Devin slid to a halt in front of one of the bookcases. His hand ran along the books and he pulled one out, handing it to Davy. He then searched to find the statue that he remembered.

"That book and this statue, Davy. This is what she was focused on." Devin looked up as Brock approached.

"Devin? What is going on?"

"Davy doesn't think this has anything to do with London. He asked if Deri had had any trouble here before she left. I can remember one time her saying something had bothered her in town but she didn't say what. Then just before she left, she was looking at that book and that statue."

"Those? They were gifts from someone I did a painting job for. It was a fire job if I remember. The office had burnt." Brock paled. "You know, there was a rumour that he had torched the office himself for insurance but that could never be proven. He was rich enough and powerful enough to buy off someone if he wanted to. Is he the one?"

"He might be, Brock. Let me have his name and I'll look into him. I gather he's still in town."

"He is and is trying to muscle his way onto the council. That has never worked. Not yet. But it could happen. I suspect that he is behind some of what is going on in town. I still say that Lucy Logan wasn't the only one after Barnabas and Bruce."

"You think that, Brock? You never said that." Bruce looked at his friend, a frown in place.

"I do, Bruce. It's just a gut feeling and I have no proof."

"I know your gut feelings. They are usually right on."

Chapter 43

Will looked up from his desk work as Davy tapped at his door and then motioned him in. He sat back, waiting for Davy to sit and then speak. Davy paced for a few moments before he sat.

"Will? I had a thought. Rather, Devin and I had a thought, and I would like to run with it, if I may."

"And that would be?" Will had learned to trust Davy's instincts, honed as an undercover officer.

"It has never made sense about London, has it?" Davy watched as Will shook his head. "I asked Devin if Deri had ever mentioned anything at all. He said she was upset, concerned, bothered by something that had happened in town during her last year of university. Before she left for London, he found her studying a book and statue in her father's office. Long story short? They were given to Brock by a customer. Only the customer may not be on the up and up."

Will nodded. "I had the same thought, that something had happened here and with Deri moving back, it has raised itself again. Who?"

"Who? The man?" Davy named him and Will stared at him for a moment before he nodded.

"I can see that. He's always been on my radar. Except I have never had any evidence. Brock mentioned that it was suspected he torched his own office?"

"He did. I'm pulling files and evidence on that. Talking to the fire marshal who is still on staff. I also asked Emma to research him."

"Good. She'll find information that we never could. Now, where do you plan to go with this? How far?"

"As far as I need to. I want to find Dallas and Deri. They don't deserve to disappear. Nor do their families and friends deserve that."

"Okay. Keep me updated. Spread your work among the others if you can. I know there will be cases that you can't. Work with the abduction people as well. Public relations is preparing a statement to go out too."

"Good. All eyes are what we need. I haven't heard from Storm."

"No, and he will contact you if he has anything. That means there is no word on the street or that he has not been able to verify it."

"My thoughts. Thanks, Will." Davy walked away, Will's eyes following him before he looked down at his paperwork. He sighed. Some days, it just didn't suit him to be chief of police as much as he loved his work. His pen back in his hand, he worked away until a sudden thought had him on his feet, his pen thrown down. He searched for Davy.

"Davy?" He paused in Davy's office doorway. "What we were talking about? There's another name that you need to look at. A good friend of his. Actually, a council member. We always wondered how he was able to afford to run." Will gave the name and Davy looked at him in shock.

"I just came across that name. How did you do that?"

Will grinned. "Comes from living here all my life." He walked away, intent on finding a patrol officer and sending him or her into the downtown area, in particular, to that very building, to sit out front for a while.

Davy looked up at long last, to find one of the techs in front of him.

"Tracy? What do you have?"

"You had us working on the evidence or what we could from Deri's car? I found this. I'm not sure if it's hers or not." She handed over an evidence bag.

"What is this?"

"A flash drive. It's designed to look like this, a lipstick. But I don't remember Deri wearing any lipstick."

"No, she doesn't." Davy grinned. "I would have seen evidence of Dallas' face if she had."

Tracy grinned. "That serious?"

"It is. They're engaged."

"Wonderful. I know Deri from church and school. We were in a lot of the same classes. They make a cute couple."

"They do. Now, did you look at the drive?"

"I did. I have a report printing at the moment. I wanted to show you this first."

"Okay. Let's go get your report and see what we have."

"You won't like it. I can tell you that already. It shows a plan to set Deri up for a fall. Just why or how I'm not sure. I hadn't read all the way through it. I left that for you."

Chapter 44

Neither Brock nor Beth was getting much sleep. They laid awake at night, hands held, their hearts praying for their daughter and her beloved Dallas. Devin had taken to driving around the town, Kara usually with him, searching for his sister. Anywhere that he could think to search he did. The building family was searching as well. Not a sighting had been reported.

Davy had read through the report from the thumb drive and grew angry as well as more afraid for his friend. These people are vicious, he thought. First an arson. Then blackmail and extortion. Now more than likely kidnapping. Was murder next? He prayed that it wasn't but didn't hold out much hope. His faith was stretching, he knew, and had made a point of going to their pastor, Daniel, asking for specific prayer. He had been assured that he was being prayed for and if he needed to talk, to come and find Daniel.

A week had gone by. Storm had tracked down Davy one day, shaking his head.

"I just don't get it, Davy. I have no word." The two men were seated in a local diner, Storm the very picture of a down and outer getting a needed meal.

"I know. I was hoping that you had. Is the hit still out on Dallas?"

"It is." Davy grew quiet, his demeanour changing more to the down and outer as a customer entered. His voice lowered. "That man there? He's been asking about Dallas. Seemed too interested in finding him. I hid from him."

"Good. Now, keep your eyes open." Davy stood, check in hand. "Enjoy your meal, my friend. Stay safe." He walked away, Storm looking up at him over his lowered brows, watching as the customer he had pinpointed followed Davy. He arose, walking with the shuffling step that he had perfected, following the two. He intentionally ran into the man and began to abjectly apologize, the man's wallet lifted and then returned to his pocket.

Davy watched from his vehicle, shaking his head. Whatever Storm was up to, he prayed that his friend stayed safe. It would soon be time to talk with him again, but for now, he had work to do. He drove away, his mind already on the searches that he needed to do.

Storm stopped in the doorway of a broken-down building, his keen eyes searching the area before he opened the paper that he had pulled from the man's wallet. It was as he suspected. This man was the hitman. He needed to find Davy but had no idea where he would be. He searched for coins, heading for a payphone, calling Davy's number and leaving a message for him. Now, Storm thought, things might just get ahead.

Davy listened to the message, then was on his feet, heading for the detective who had been looking for this very man.

———

"Earl? I have word on that man you were looking for. He was in the diner that I was in earlier."

Earl leaned back in his chair. "He was? Do you have confirmation of this? Of course, you do. You wouldn't be here if you didn't." Earl was on his feet, reaching for his jacket. "Where do I find him?"

"This is where he is staying. Take backup with you." Davy headed back for his office, stopping in the break room for a fresh mug of coffee. Tracy was standing there, staring at the microwave.

"Tracy? A lab experiment?" Davy grinned as she spun.

"No." She laughed at him. "Just my muffin. And a lot of muddled thoughts. I have no idea what to make of them."

"Write them down. Let me know if I can help with anything." Davy turned, mug in hand, ready to leave when Tracy spoke.

"It's about Deri. Something is bugging me about that thumb drive. Why was it there? Did they not see it? It was right out in the open."

Davy spun. "You didn't tell me that. So the information may be a setup, designed to change our track of investigation. That makes sense. I haven't been able to find anything on that information that was on it, and I should have."

"We were played, Davy. Why had we not found her car before? Where was it hidden? And when did that woman arrive in Ontario? Do we know that?"

Davy pointed a finger at her. "Bingo. Just what I was thinking. Can I borrow you from the lab for a couple of days?"

Tracy grinned. "All ready asked and granted. I was coming to find you next." She grabbed her muffin from the microwave and her bottle of juice. "Where are we working?"

"In board room number one. I have the evidence from that fire years ago. We need to start searching back through it. As long as you're okay with that?"

"I am. I want to find her and this may be one way to do that."

Chapter 45

Davy walked towards the front door of Brock's house later that same day. Tracy is good, he thought. She sifted through everything so quickly, organized it, and then found this. He looked down at the copy of the photo he had in a folder. Hopefully, Brock could give some insight on this.

Beth watched him, seeing the fatigue in his steps.

"Davy? You're in time for dinner, such as it is. Come in. Set aside your worries and your work. It's what we are trying to do tonight. Join us for a meal."

Davy looked up with a smile. "I would be glad to, Beth. It's been a long day."

"And you're not getting a lot of sleep."

"None of us are. We're working on this, Beth, as hard as we can. I have some information that I need to go over with Brock. But first? A home-cooked meal sounds good."

"Neasa dusted off her chef skills and made us some casseroles. They are delicious. Only we don't feel much like eating, do we?"

"No. As Brock would say, we eat, we pray, then we talk."

An hour later, Davy rose to help clear the table. They had eaten. They had spent time in prayer. Now it was time to talk.

"Davy?" Brock sounded hopeful. "You have news?"

"I have some information that I need to speak with you about. That fire all those years ago? It was covered up well. The fire marshal at the time was bought off. We have determined that. Tracy from the lab has been working with me. It didn't take long to run that down. He's being pulled in for questioning. It was as you thought. Arson."

"It was? That was our gut feeling. Did he set it himself?"

Davy hesitated and then nodded. "That's what we finding out. He's disappeared. Something about a relative out of town who is sick and he's the only one who could go."

"Convenient." Beth snorted at that.

"Too convenient, I would say." Brock reached for the folder being handed him. "What this?"

"Open it. Look at it. And then talk to me."

Brock stared down at the photo, his face growing grim.

"I know him. He's the man's brother. He was killed in an accident years ago." He looked up. "Did he set the fire and then was killed to hide it?"

"That's what we're thinking. I'm working on that assumption, pulling the file on the accident. Unfortunately, it seems as if the same officer was involved in reporting both cases."

"A dirty cop? And he's dead now, right?"

"He is. Hit and run that was never solved."

"This just gets better and better. How far did this man go? And what does he want from Deri?"

"That we don't know. We have some working assumptions but nothing confirmed. Is Devin around?"

"No. He and Kara had a meeting at the church that they had to be at. He wasn't sure what time he would be home."

"Okay. Have him come into the detachment in the morning. I need to speak with him." Davy paused. "That book?"

"The one that I was given? You want to take it and the statue? Let me get them." Brock headed for his office and returned. The statue slipped from his hand and hit the floor, breaking into pieces. "I'm sorry, Davy. It just slipped."

Davy was on his knees, gathering up the pieces when his hands stilled. He held up a key.

"What's this?"

"A key? I never knew that it was there." Brock turned abruptly to the book and began leaving through it. "There are words underlined in here that I never noticed. I never read it, never really looked at it. I had planned to throw it out at some point, only never got that far."

"It's a good thing that you didn't. Let me take these and put Tracy to work on it. She'll figure it out, I have no doubt."

Chapter 46

Early the next morning, Deri struggled against the man who was holding her, trying to force her into a vehicle. That she was leaving Dallas behind she could not accept. She needed to free herself and then find help to free him.

The man cursed at her as she struggled, an arm around her and his other hand covering her mouth. Her mind went blank for a moment and then Devin's self-defence training kicked in. Her heel hammered down as hard as it could on one foot and then the other before she bent her knee to kick at his with her foot and then scrape the foot down his shin. Her hand found his thumb and pulled it back from his hand as far and as hard as she could. Her head hit backwards, finding his nose.

The man's cursing change to a howl of pain and his grip loosened enough that Deri could free herself. She dropped to her knees for a moment before she pushed herself upright to run. Her feet thudded loudly on the empty sidewalk as she ran, her breath coming in rough gasps.

Deri finally paused, a hand to her face, as she turned, searching behind her. Where was he? Had she managed to escape him? She faintly heard running footsteps and took off again. Deri paused once more outside of a broken-down building. Feeling an arm around her once more, her mouth opened to scream before a hand was slapped across it. She was pulled backwards into the shadows, fighting at her attacker.

"Deri! Stop! It's a friend. I'm Storm." Storm's voice finally managed to reach through the absolute panic and terror that gripped her. She stopped her fighting, her energy spent. "If I take away my hand, you won't scream?" Storm waited until she shook her head. "Okay, Deri. I'm going to take you somewhere safe. We can talk later." He reached for her hand to pull her into the building.

Deri was too afraid to look around much. Storm led her to a bulky buildout that seemed to be attached to the wall.

"It's okay, Deri. This is hollow. I'll lift you up and over and you can hide in there. You'll find water and blankets. I stash my supplies there." He looked around. "Where's Dallas?"

"I don't know. They separated us last night. I think he's still in the building but I don't know for sure."

"What building?" Davy waited patiently, his eyes gentle as he did so. "Deri, what building?"

"Oh! The old State building. You know the one?"

"I do. I'll search it but first up you go." He lifted her up, waiting until she had her balance before he removed his hands. "Down you go. Don't come out for anyone but me, Davy, Dallas, or Will. Understand? No matter what you hear. If no one comes in twelve hours, hop out and run. Head for the shelter or the police detachment. The shelter's closest but you're safest with the police."

"Thank you, Storm. Will you be alright?" Her voice was low, barely audible to him.

"I will." He turned at a noise. "Hush now. No more talking." He was across the room in rapid steps, down on the rough pallet with a blanket pulled up and over him as if he were asleep. He watched through narrowed eyes as the man entered, searching for Deri, he suspected before the man's attention turned to him.

A foot nudged at Storm and when he didn't respond, nudged harder.

"Wake up. I need to talk to you."

Storm moved the blanket down a fraction and peered at the man, his eyes narrowed as if he had a hangover.

"Waddaya want? I'm trying to sleep." His voice had taken on a roughened tone to it.

"Wake up. I need to know if you saw a woman come in here."

Storm pulled the blanket back over his head. "No woman. Just me. Now got outta here. I'm sleeping."

The man pulled the blanket back to Storm's shout to leave it alone.

"I have good money to give you. I need to find her."

"Not my problem, man. Get outta here." Storm pulled the blanket back up, a snore coming as he pretended to sleep, all the while watching through the opening he had managed to keep.

He watched the man search the room before he stomped off, anger emanating from him. Storm waited and then was on his feet, silently moving across the room, and out of it, to watch the man walk away, kicking at whatever got in his way.

Good, Storm thought. Let him get away and then I can get Deri away. He looked over as he heard noise and Joe appeared.

"Storm? You look like you could use a coffee this morning." Joe greeted Storm as if he was really a down-and-out derelict needing a handout.

"I could." Storm kept to his character, the roughened voice not changing. "Glad of it, in fact." He sipped at the cardboard cup of coffee. "I just had a visitor that you need to check out."

"Is that right?" Joe memorized the description. "After someone was he?"

"He was. That Deri. She escaped him."

"She has?" Joe looked around, keeping his hope down that Storm knew where she was.

"I have her hidden. Come back in about an hour or so. Just to make sure that he doesn't come back."

Joe walked away without a word. Storm watched him and then moved away himself. He needed some things and he had to get them between now and when Joe returned.

He returned quickly, his purchases dropped down for a moment on his pallet. He looked around. No one had been in, he thought. He walked over to where he had hidden Deri.

"Deri. Don't say anything. I have a friend coming back to get you shortly. I'll have you out and dressed in what I found for you by then. Just stay put for now. Tap on the wall if you understand." He heard the faint tap and smiled. A lady with a head on her shoulders. Dallas, you have a wonderful lady here. Now to get her to safety and then find you.

Chapter 47

An hour later, Joe returned as promised, his patrol vehicle at the door, lights flashing. He entered, finding Storm watching him, a lady with him. At least, he thought it was a lady, but he wasn't quite sure. She was dressed in a ratty long coat, a scarf wrapped around her head and face, rough almost-worn-out boots on her feet.

"Come on. Let's go. Into the car, you two." Joe shoved at them, forcing them through the door and into the back of his vehicle. If anyone had been watching closely, they would have seen that he barely touched them, Storm giving the impression that they had been roughly treated.

Joe drove off, watchful, seeing the man appear as he did so. A quick word on the radio and he saw officers moving in, the man turning in surprise and then trying to run.

"We got him, Storm." Joe glanced back, finding the woman's eyes on him. "Deri? Is it Deri?" He waited until she gave a reluctant nod. "I'm Joe. I would have been one that Storm said to wait for. Storm, keep in character, will you? I need to take you in and put you into an interrogation room. You too, Deri. We'll need your statement. And we'll need any information from you that you can give to find Dallas."

"The old State building. We were there. They separated us last night and then brought me out this morning. I have no idea why. Please? Will you check there?"

"We will. As soon as I can get you two to safety, I'll head over there. I have a team waiting with a search warrant. Thanks for your heads up, Storm."

"Just find him, Joe. That's all the thanks that I need. It's been too long." Storm turned to watch Deri. "Was he okay?"

"I don't know. They kept us apart most of the time, only letting us be together when we ate. And he wasn't eating. Only sipping at the water. Please? Find him?" Tears welled in her eyes, tears that she was unable to control.

"We'll do that." Joe parked and then opened the back door. "All right, you two. Out of the vehicle." He punched in his code and then pulled open the back door. "Head for the small conference room instead, Storm. Take Deri with you."

Heading for Davy's office, Joe detoured for a moment, stopping in Wills' doorway.

"Will?" When Will looked up, Joe spoke quietly. "I have Deri. Storm found her or she found him. They're in the small conference room."

Will was on his feet. "Dallas?"

"Not yet, but Deri told us where we should be able to find him. I'm heading that way now with backup and search warrants."

"Good. Come find me when you are back. Davy?"

"Heading his way now."

"Go on. Head on out. I'll find him." Will walked rapidly towards Davy's office, a spring in his step that hadn't been there in the last few days. He watched Davy hard at work, shuffling through the papers spread out in front of him, and making notes. "Davy?"

Davy looked up, a frown on his face at being interrupted. "Will? You look happy."

"I am, sort of. We have Deri."

Davy was on his feet, in front of Will. "The hospital?"

"No. Here. She's in the conference room with Storm."

"Storm? He came through?"

"I would suspect so. Joe brought them in. He's heading for a building that Deri says they were held in. Hopefully, they will find him."

"And alive and in one piece." Davy hesitated at the door, his eyes trained on it before he spoke. "God heard, didn't He?"

"He did and in His timing. We can't forget that fact, Davy. God answers as He does and in His timing."

Davy turned the doorknob, opening the door slowly and entering. He frowned again as he saw only Storm, hearing Will stop in surprise beside him even as the door closed behind them.

Storm turned, a smile breaking out on his face before he pointed to a corner of the room. Davy moved so he could see it before he moved forward, crouching down in front of Deri. Deri had tucked herself into a small huddle in the corner, her legs folded under her, her arms wrapped around herself. She watched Davy closely.

"Deri? I am so glad to see you. Would you like to step over here and have a chair?" Davy waited, his hand out for her to take.

Deri studied him and then his hand before she was on her feet, moving past him, stopping as she saw Will. A small cry sounded from her and she was across the room, flinging herself at Will, her tears flowing. A friend, she thought. Someone who understands and can help.

Will's arms closed around her and he shook his head at the other two men.

"Some tea, I think, Davy, will help and maybe some crackers or something."

"On it." Davy was away and back in short order, finding Deri seated at the table, the scarf and coat discarded. He saw the bruising on her face and flinched. What did they do to you, Deri?

"Here you go, Deri." Will sat beside her, pushing the tray towards her. "Drink your tea. Eat some crackers. Then we'll talk."

"We will? Dallas?" Her voice was rough and tired sounded, but she refused to reach for the tray until Will spoke.

"Joe's gone after him. He'll bring him here when he finds him. But Dallas would want you to eat, wouldn't he?"

"I guess. Maybe." Deri stared down at the tea and crackers. "We didn't have much to eat. Only once a day. And fast food at that. Do you know how much I hate fast food?"

Will grinned. "I know, Deri. You have never liked it all that much. Now eat and then we talk."

Chapter 48

Standing in front of the State building, Joe shook his head. Who would have thought to look here? It was a well-known landmark in town, the family who had built it some of the town founders. At present, it was shuttered and abandoned. Without just cause or a search warrant, they had not been able to enter it. He turned as a fellow officer approached.

"How sure are we, Joe?"

"We have Deri's word but he could have been moved at any time overnight or up until now. Ready?"

"We are. Let's move. We want to find Dallas and get him home."

"We all do." Joe walked up the broad slate steps and knocked, not expecting an answer. He tried the doorknob, which turned under his hand, shoving at the door. He blinked at the low lights. "We'll need our flashlights, people."

"Right here."

Taking the light handed him, Joe began the slow methodical search that was needed. They found nothing.

"This is strange, Joe. He was here."

"I know." Joe spun in a circle. "You know, there are secret rooms here. On this floor. I toured it once when I first came on the force." Joe was rapidly moving to what would have been called the parlour. "In here. This bookshelf. Now, let's see if we can move it."

Searching for a latch to release a door, they finally found it, pushing at the decorative knob. The door swung open silently, showing a dark room behind it.

Joe studied the floor. "It's been opened recently. I can tell that. Let's see what's in here." His light shone around the room, coming back to a huddled form on the floor. He sprang forward, onto his knees, reaching to turn the body over. "It's Dallas. He's alive. Let's get him out of here."

Willing hands reached to help as Dallas was carried gently from the room and to the outdoors. A paramedic team had been assigned to wait and hurried forward with the stretcher that soon held Dallas.

Joe stood back, relief on his face before he looked around. "I'm riding with him. Stan, you have lead here. Get what warrants that you think we need. You know the drill."

"I do, Joe. Keep us updated."

"I will." Joe climbed aboard the rig, watching Dallas closely before his phone was out. "Davy? We have Dallas. I'm heading in with him."

"You have him? Praise the Lord. I suspect I'll be there as well." Davy pocketed his phone, his eyes on Will as he nodded. Will's eyes slid closed as he breathed a sigh of relief.

Davy pulled out a chair beside Deri, his eyes on her. He could see Storm silently slipping away from the room and nodded. It's what he does.

"Deri? Can you look at me?" Davy waited until she did. "You did good, Deri. You were right."

"I was?" Deri was confused for a moment until hope lit up her face. "You found Dallas?"

"We did. Joe's heading to the hospital with him. Let us get your statement and then we'll head there."

Her statement given, Deri paced the room, unable to sit, unable to stay in one place. She just wanted to be with Dallas. Lord, thank You. I don't know how he is, but You do. You have brought us out of that situation. Only, who was it? Lord, You know. Help the people here to find those responsible. Fatigue was hitting her in waves and she finally sat, her head rested on her folded arms, her eyes on the doorway.

Davy looked up as Tracy reappeared in his office, shopping bags in hand.

"Here you go, Davy. I found what I think she'll like. At least, I hope that she will." Tracy held out the bags.

Davy was on his feet, pointing to the hallway.

"Let's go. I need either you or Trish with me." Trish was one of the female detectives and now stood outside his doorway, waiting. "Trish? You have a few moments?"

"I do. I would make time if I had to. Tracy?"

Tracy grinned. "New clothing for Deri. I'll take her old stuff. I doubt that she'll want to keep it anyway."

"No, I doubt that she will." Trish tapped at the door and then entered the room, finding Deri on her feet, hope on her face. "Hi, Deri. I'm Trish. And I think that you know Tracy."

Deri nodded before she looked at Tracy. "Tracy? It's been so long. This is where you work?"

Tracy grinned at her. "It is. I'm one of the techs. Trish here is one of the detectives. Now, we need you to come with us." Tracy held up a hand at Deri's protest. "We're just taking you to our locker room, letting you shower, wash your hair, and change into some brand-new clothing. I know if it was me and I was heading to find my fellow, I would want to be clean and in clean clothing. And your old clothing? We'll dump it into a bag and I'll get rid of it for you."

Showered and dressed in fresh clothing, Deri reached to hug first Trish and then Tracy.

"Thank you, ladies, whichever one of you it was who thought of this."

Trish laughed even as she opened the door. "Thank Davy. He's the one who sent Tracy out. And before you even offer, don't. He won't take any money for it. He saw too much on the streets to want to be repaid."

"He did? I guess he did. Storm?" Deri hesitated as she watched Davy heading her way, jacket on and keys in hand.

"Storm? Oh, him." Trish waved a hand. "Don't worry about him. He's a survivor. He'll have moved his quarters already."

Davy watched Deri closely, seeing the fatigue in her face as well as a loss of innocence in her eyes. This should not have happened, Lord. She shouldn't have been put through this. I wonder what all they said to her that she didn't tell me. I am sure there were words that she can't or won't repeat. Not until she sees Dallas and knows that he is safe.

Chapter 49

Doc Andrews looked around as he heard the commotion heading his way and stood to walk to the hallway from the office that he was using. The Emergency Department had been relatively quiet for a while and he had been catching up on his paperwork.

"Doc?" The paramedic at the head of the stretcher.

"In there." Doc pointed at one of the rooms. "What do we have?"

"We have Dallas. Can't tell you much though."

Doc peered at him before moving rapidly to the stretcher.

"Dallas? How?"

The paramedic shrugged. "I don't know. We were asked to stand by at a site and the officers brought him out."

"Okay." Doc helped to shift Dallas to the other stretcher before he moved in. He studied his young friend and shook his head. "Dallas, what have you done? I know you're safe but where were you and what happened?"

He began his assessment, wincing himself as he found the spots that Dallas moved away from his touch.

"Imaging, Sue. Blood work. And then we'll assess again." He looked around at the nurse. "Any word on Deri?"

"Deri? Should there be?" Sue looked at him, a question on her face.

"She's his fiancée. She's been missing too."

"Oh! I didn't realize that." She looked around at footsteps. "Here's Davy. Maybe he has word."

"Doc?" Davy nodded at Sue before he approached the stretcher. "How is he?"

"Bruises. Tenderness over the kidneys and spleen. He's not awakened." Doc stood for a moment, his eyes on his young friend. "Deri?"

"She's in another room here, waiting for you to assess her." Davy didn't say much more and Doc didn't ask.

Doc stood watching Deri before he moved to stand beside her. She jumped as he appeared, fear on her face as she looked up.

"You're safe, Deri. I won't let anyone hurt you." Doc watched as she relaxed. "Now, let's see how you are."

"I'm tired, Doc. And hungry. I didn't get a lot of sleep or a lot of food." Deri watched as Sue drew the blood for the work up Doc had requested. "Dallas?"

"Let's get you looked at. Dallas is here. I've seen him." Doc watched her closely as her eyes slid closed and a single tear trickled down her face. "Once I am satisfied that you are okay and that he can see you, I'll take you over there."

"I'm his next of kin, Doc. We changed that to each other." She stared down at her ring. "We're engaged, but it sure hasn't been a happy time."

"No, I don't think that it has been. Okay. Lay back down, Deri. We'll get the blood work run and then I'll be back. Davy's here if you need him."

"No, it's okay." She looked up, concern on her face. "Mom? Dad? Devin?"

"Davy was calling them. Or else Will was heading that way." Doc watched as her eyes closed and she slept. "Let her sleep, Sue. She needs that."

Will tapped at Brock's kitchen door and then entered with the welcome of a long-time friend. He found the three in the kitchen, their lunch in front of them but he could tell that they had not been eating.

"Will?" Brock was on his feet, fear on his face as he faced Will.

Will held up a hand, a smile on his face that had the three frowning.

"I need you all to come with me."

"Will? Deri?" Beth rose, hope on her face.

Will nodded. "We have her. I won't go into details but we have her and she's at the hospital."

Beth stared at him before tears started. "Oh, thank God. What time?"

"I'm sorry. I'm not sure what you mean." Will was puzzled and shared a look with Brock.

"What time did you find her?"

"Oh, that. I would say around seven this morning."

"Praise the Lord! That's when I felt a peace that she would be home today." Beth almost ran for her coat before she spun. "Dallas?"

"Him too. We have them safe and under guard." Will waited as they sorted themselves out. "I'll drive you."

Devin shook his head. "I'll meet you there. I want to find Kara." He was gone before Will could stop them.

Beth and Brock sat impatiently in the waiting room. Doc had found them, gave a brief update on Deri, and then walked away.

"Beck." Brock pulled out his phone. "I need to call Beck."

"Yes, we do." She looked up as she felt someone near her. "Actually, you don't. He's here."

"What?" Brock was dialling his brother, frowning as he heard the phone ringing near him. He looked down as Beth's hand covered his.

"He's here, Brock."

Brock looked up and then was on his feet, his brother's hug tight. Bonnie sat beside Beth, her arms around the other woman.

"It's true? Deri's here?"

Brock stepped back from his brother. "It is. Will came to find us about an hour or so ago. Dallas is here too."

"He is? Oh, wonderful news! Devin called me, just saying that Deri was here and would we come? Breck and Neasa are on their way, I suspect. I had to leave a voice mail for them."

Davy watched them from where he stood beside Will.

"We're not out of the woods yet, Will."

"No, we're not. Right now, I want officers with them. Doc hasn't said how long that they'll be in, but even when they go home, I want officers with them. Make sure that Dallas goes to Brock's. Take his keys and get what he needs. I've spoken with Susan and Sean. They want to head this way but I told them no. Not now. They could well be used to draw Dallas out again."

"That they could. This hurts, you know." Davy walked away, heading back to his office, leaving Will staring after him, nodding.

Chapter 50

Dallas stirred, rolling to his side, a groan coming from him as he hit sore ribs. His hand found the spot, even as a hand touched his face. No, he thought. It can't be Deri. We're not together. They made sure of that.

"Dallas?"

A soft beloved voice whispered his name before a kiss landed on his cheek. He stirred again. His hand reached for the one on his cheek.

"Dallas? Please? Open your eyes. We're safe." Deri bent over his bed, desperate for him to awaken.

"Deri?" He had to clear his throat, his voice rough from disuse. "Are you okay?"

"I am. We're safe, Dallas. You're at Mom and Dad's." Deri slipped to her knees, her hand held tight in his. "Please, Dallas?"

Dallas' eyes cracked open and then closed against the low light before he opened them again, finding Deri's face close to his.

"Deri? You're sure?" It wasn't that Dallas didn't trust what she was saying but that he had trouble believing it.

"I am." Deri gave a soft, tear-filled laugh. "You're safe. I got away and then Davy had someone go and find you."

"He did." Dallas' eyes flickered open and closed as he drifted off to sleep.

Deri watched him for a while before she reached to kiss him and then rose, heading for the downstairs. Her father watched her as she approached him, assessing her, heartbroken at the look on her face.

"Deri?"

"It's okay, Dad. Dallas was just awake." She walked into her father's hug. "I love you, Dad. I'm sorry that you were worried."

"Not your fault, baby girl. Here. I know it's early but I have some tea and toast ready for you."

Deri slipped into a chair at the kitchen table, eyeing the soft yellows and creams with a touch of brown that her mother had used to decorate.

"I didn't think that I would see this again. Ever."

"I know. We didn't think you would either." Brock sat at his usual spot, his eyes on his mug. "I won't ask, Deri, as I know Davy and his team will need to speak with you again."

"Davy said I could talk to you. He encouraged it. Said we needed to. I wanted to wait until Dallas is ready, but that might not be for a while." She sighed, looking at the clock. "You're off to work soon, Dad. And I need to spend some time on the piano. I need that therapy. We'll talk tonight."

"That what your Mom and I thought. Is it alright if we have Beck and his family and Bruce and his?"

"Please. They need to hear this. Can you ask Buckley and Locklin? We need their guidance as a pastor. I know Daniel will be around, but Dallas needs his friends." She looked up and her father drew in his breath at the look in her eyes. She had aged, he thought, and not in a way that he would have wanted.

"We can arrange that. A light supper, I think your mother will arrange. I'll be home as soon as I can." He rose, a kiss dropped on her head and then walked away, to stand outside near his van, sorrow rising in him as well as anger, anger that he knew he needed to turn over to God. Lord, please help my baby girl to return to her walk with You. I don't know what she went through but whatever it is, it has to affect that.

Dallas watched Deri that afternoon, finally on his feet. Beth had fed him and then sent him to find Deri, concern on her face as she watched how slowly he was moving. He finally approached Deri to drop down beside her at the piano.

"Okay, love?" His finger lightly touched the keys.

Deri shrugged. "I really don't know how I feel. Or how I am to feel." She shifted so that she could watch him. "How about you?"

"I'm sore and weak, but I'll get there. I'm glad we're alive and free." He watched her as she nodded, a shuttered look on her face for a moment. "Deri? What did they do?"

She leaned against him, her arm wrapping around his. "We need to talk about that, Dallas. And before we talk to Mom and Dad."

"It was that bad?"

She didn't respond for a moment. "In a way. They threatened to kill you in front of me. Then threatened to send me somewhere. Only I have no idea where. I think that's what that man was up to when he pulled me from the house and I escaped."

Chapter 51

Deri's mind drifted back, back to New Year's Eve. They had been at the building family get-together. She had been welcomed, that she knew, as part of the growing family. Dallas had been on top of the world, she thought, as she watched him with his friends. This is good for him, she had thought. He needs them and they need him. They have been through so much together. Deri herself had been welcomed by the ladies. The little ones were asleep in their own beds and she missed seeing Heath and Hannah.

They had headed home after midnight, the dark blue night sky showing the moon and the brilliant stars. They hadn't talked but then they hadn't needed to. Dallas had pulled to a stop in the driveway, his eyes on the garage door before he came around to open her door. She had stepped out of the vehicle and into his arms, his kiss welcome on her lips.

They had barely made a move towards the front door when a man had appeared in their way. Dallas had shoved Deri behind him even as he stood a step backwards. He had felt Deri's hands grasping the back of his jacket before he heard a soft cry from her. Dallas had twisted in such a way that he could watch the man in front of him and then search behind him

His hands raised as he saw Deri held by a masked man, a knife to her throat. He could feel the terror that she felt, that was a given. He had been forced back into his vehicle, Deri taken to another, and made to drive away. Dallas' heart sank as he saw the motor vehicle wrecker's in front of him and he was forced to drive through the gates, gates that swung shut behind him. They will never find my vehicle, will they, Lord? Protect my love, please, dear Lord?

Deri watched as Dallas was shoved towards a second vehicle that waited in front of them. Her wrists had been bound and she was unable to escape. Even if she had tried, the threat of harm to Dallas kept her still. There was no way that she would do anything to harm him.

Dallas groaned to himself as he saw the building they were brought to. The State building, he thought. There is no way that it could be searched. He moved away from the hand shoving at him, turning to seek for Deri. She was behind him, protesting at being forced to move forward. Deri, he thought, please just go along with them for now. Let me think through a way to get you free. Lord? Please? Keep us safe. Help us to get away.

Dallas was shoved into one room, Deri into another. She protested at that, but to a slamming door as it was shut and locked. She pounded at it, yelling for them to come back. To unlock the door and let her go to Dallas. When that didn't work, Deri paused her onslaught on the door and stood, back to it, looking around the room, what she could see in the darkness. The windows, she thought, and ran for them, trying to force the water-swollen wooden windows and unable to do that. Breaking them was an option but it would be too noisy, she decided.

She had finally huddled down in a corner, her knees drawn up, trying to keep warm. There was some heat but not a lot. Deri's head went to her knees and she slept. She was awakened the next morning by a rough shove with a boot. Drawn to her feet, she was dragged from the room to the kitchen and pushed down into a chair, a plate of toast and water set before her. She stared at it, refusing to eat.

Dallas shuffled towards the table, an arm around his abdomen. He too stared at the toast and water and finally began to eat. He could sense Deri sending him glances before she too ate. He hurt, he decided. He had fought hard to get to her, unable to do so for the blows that were directed at him. A vicious blow to his jaw had taken him down and out, his body sprawled on its back, his head turned to the side. The man stood over him, shaking his head.

This went on for days. Neither one was questioned or asked for anything at first. Then, the questions and comments began with Deri.

"Where is the paper?"

"What paper?" Deri was confused. "I don't know what you want."

The same line of questioning had gone on for a couple of days before it changed tone.

"Where's the key?"

"What key? I don't know what you are talking about." She bit at her lip, ducking from the hand directed towards her. "Please. Can I see Dallas?

"Not a chance. Never again, little lady. As of noon tomorrow, you're on a flight out of here. You're not coming back." She had stared at the man in horror as he sneered at her.

Left on her own, Deri had paced. Lord, how do I get away? And how do I get Dallas away? He didn't come out for his breakfast this morning. Is he okay, dear Lord? Please, please, protect him. Free him. I don't care about myself. I just want him free.

Chapter 52

Dallas thought back to what had happened. He didn't remember a whole lot, the men had seen to that. His body hurt, all over, he thought. All he could remember was trying to get to Deri. He had heard her voice in protest and then in pain and had hammered at the door locked in front of him. Dallas had finally been unable to rise, his body only taking so much. That had been that last day, from what Deri had just said, the day before she disappeared. He never knew that she had escaped and that he had been moved to the secret room.

He had roused in the hospital, barely awake as he spoke with Davy, giving what he could of a statement. Which wasn't much, he acknowledged. Davy had nodded, told him to sleep, and that he would catch up with him later.

Dallas listened as Deri told him about that last morning. She had not been able to sleep that night, standing instead staring out the window, trying her best to come up with a plan. She had finally just started to pray, asking that God would help her to escape and that He would keep Dallas alive so that he could be found.

Deri had been pulled from that room in the early dawn of the morning, the sky barely breaking with the light. He wrapped an arm around her as she described fighting the man, escaping, and then fleeing. Dallas breathed a sigh of relief as he heard had Storm had found her and then hidden her.

"Storm said he would." Dallas kissed her temple.

"I know. I just didn't expect him to appear as he did. He had me hid in the room that he was using. I could hear voices but didn't move at all." Deri began to laugh. "He found me this long ratty coat, a scarf, and worn-out boots to put on. Joe, I think it was, appeared and then whisked us away." She blinked rapidly. "When I saw Will, I think I lost it. I know that he hugged me just like my Dad would have."

"He would have. He's a good friend to your family." Dallas paused, his eyes on the spot where the Christmas tree had stood. "Do you have any idea what their plans for you were?"

Deri hesitated a long time before she nodded. "I think they were sending me out of the country for some reason. They didn't say what but from their looks it wasn't for my good."

"No, I doubt that it was. They didn't seem to really know what they were doing or wanted. Somewhat incompetent, I would think."

"They were. The questions that they asked me? They didn't make a lot of sense." Deri spun on the bench to face him. "What paper? And what key?"

Brock startled them as he spoke from behind them.

"We found a key in that statue, Deri. And the book had underlining in it that I had never noticed. Davy took both and was working on them."

"Is there a lock in that building the key would fit?" Dallas turned to Brock.

———

229

Brock shrugged. "I have no idea. I am sure between Joe and Davy they'll figure it out." He watched them for a few moments, seeing the changes in both of them. "Mom has supper ready, Deri, if you're up to it."

"Thanks, Dad. We'll be out soon." She shared a look with Dallas. "Dad, are Uncle Beck and Aunt Bonnie coming?"

"They're here already as are Breck and Neasa and Bruce and his family. Buckley and Locklin are here as well."

Deri nodded, her eyes on Dallas even as she heard her father walk away.

"Deri? What are you thinking?" Dallas knew that she was thinking of something, she had that look in her eyes.

"We need to set a date, Dallas. We have talked about that. Let's not let it go too far."

His phone out and the calendar app pulled up, Dallas studied it. "We need to give it a couple of weeks. How about mid-January?"

Deri finally nodded. "That works. We'll need to speak with Daniel, I guess. He's our pastor."

"He is. Buckley would be willing to do the ceremony."

"I know. But we first need to find out what is all involved in this." She was on her feet, heading for her father's office before Dallas stopped her.

“We eat first, Deri. Your Mom did make a meal for us.”

“She did.” Deri sighed, torn between needing to eat and wanting to hunt for answers. Eating wins, she supposed.

Chapter 53

It was late the next day before Deri finally sat back from her father's computer. She had spent the day emailing the ladies from London, Emma, Branigan, and whoever else she could think of. She knew she had the answer. She just had to put it together.

Dallas had been in and out, on the phone with Davy and then Abe. He didn't like the warning both men gave him. He knew that they were at risk, particularly Deri. Just how was he to keep her safe? They had both decided, together, that they were not hiding. Not at all. They were done with that.

Deri looked up, finding Dallas perched on the edge of the desk, Breck and Barnabas on the couch, all of them watching her.

Breck's eyes narrowed. "You discovered something."

"I did. I just need to put it all together. Kara's program doesn't help other than spitting out more information."

"Print what you have. We'll put up fresh paper and work it." Barnabas was on his feet, heading for the printer. "Make copies for us all and Davy. He's heading this way, he said."

"He should just move in. He's here enough." The men smiled at her grumble, knowing that she was doing just that, grumbling.

Breck and Barnabas worked on the paper on the wall, quiet conversation between them. Dallas simply scooped Deri up into his arms and then sat back down, cuddling her close. Her head went down on his shoulder for a moment.

"Okay, love?"

She shook her head. "No. I'm not. I'm not sure that I ever will be." She blinked as she looked up at him. "You have a horrible bruise on your jaw."

Dallas winced as he touched it. "This was the last blow that I remember. I was trying to get to you and couldn't." He hugged her tighter. "What did you discover?"

"How do you know that I did?" She waited for him to speak before she sighed. "I figured out who it is. And I don't know how to tell Davy."

"Tell me what?" Davy had appeared, taking the sheaf of stapled papers that Breck handed him.

Deri looked up at him. "I figured out who it is. He's really prominent in town."

Davy said a name, watching her closely.

"That's him. He's the one who threatened me all those years ago. I didn't have proof. It would have been my word against his. I heard talk about him over the years. He's got people in London as well."

"We know, Deri. We have finally been able to piece it all together. Thanks to you."

"Me? I wasn't here?" She shared a look with Dallas. "I'm not sure that I understand."

"You were the one who directed us to the statue and the book. By the way, we found a key in the statue."

"That's what I was told. The State building?"

Davy nodded. "It was. Actually, it was to a safe in the room that we found you in, Dallas." He looked around and rose, heading for where the two men were watching him. He tapped at the paper. "This is what we were missing. All this. I take it this is what I'm holding?"

Deri nodded. "I worked it as I would a tune I was composing. I just started with the basics and went from there. Everyone that I talked to had something to add. That's a compilation of everything."

"Good. I'll take it, have it verified and work from there." Davy turned, his eyes thoughtful. "It won't be long, you two. Just a few days. We have warrants ready to serve tonight on places and people. He's one that we were serving."

"He is? But I don't understand." Deri was confused, her eyes showing it.

Dallas watched her. "It's how the detectives work, love. They take a piece of information and go from there. Just like you did. Only they need to verify it all so that their work stands up in court."

"And we have done all that. That room? I can tell you this only because it is in the warrants and the news will have it shortly. It held a wealth of information on crimes that had been going on that couldn't be proved. Including the fire at the business."

"It did?" Deri sank back against Dallas. "Then it's almost over?"

"It is, Deri. Give us a few days. Dallas, I want you to stay here. I have officers on duty outside. Your life would be worthless if you leave. An officer is working with Brock for now. I hear tell that he wants to retire and go to work for your father, Deri."

"He does? Dad does need help." She watched him walk away before she was on her feet, following him.

"Davy?"

Davy turned at her question. "Deri?"

"Storm? Is he okay?"

"He is, Deri. He is. He was asking about you today. He's coming in from the streets. He was working on this man all along. Now that we have the evidence, he can come home."

"Oh, wonderful. I was so afraid for him."

Chapter 54

Four days later, Davy stood in the doorway to the family room at Brock's, Will standing nearby. He had appeared just as they were finishing their meal. It sounded almost like a happy house, he thought, but not quite. It will never be the same, that much he knew from experience. He watched Deri and Dallas as they cuddled in the corner of the couch, Deri wrapped in a blanket, Dallas' arms tight around her. Neasa sat beside them, engaged in conversation with Deri as Breck sat on the arm of the couch, in conversation with Barnabas.

Davy studied each of the people there. Devin and Kara on the floor near the fireplace, Bruce and Elizabeth on the other side. Brock and Beth were on the other couch, Bonnie beside Beth, Beck at her feet. Buckley and Locklin were there, sharing the armchair that Beth favoured. He smiled to himself. This is what family is, isn't it?

Deri finally looked at him, her head tilting as she did so.

"Davy? I don't think you're here just for the company."

"Oh, but I am. I like this company." He grinned as she shook a finger at him. "But you are correct. I can say tonight that we have everyone arrested that we need to. We're sorting through it all but I can give you the answers, at least I hope I can, that you have been asking for." He reached to set down his mug, picking up the folder that he had set aside and opening it. He looked around. "Brock? Can we spend some time in prayer first?"

"That we can, son. I was about to suggest that." Brock led off in prayer, each one following until Beck finished.

There was silence in the room for a few moments before Davy began to speak.

"I know it's been tough on all of you. I have seen it. I have seen the changes, some good, some not so good, that have occurred. If I could have prevented any of this, then you know that I would have.

"Deri, to go back to London. I finally sorted out with the authorities there. You were correct when you surmised that you were not being taken seriously. Investigations have led to the arrest of the officer that you spoke with. He was involved in the smuggling ring. Why you were never asked? That we can't determine, only that word came from this town that you were not to be."

"I don't understand that, Davy."

"We didn't at first, but I can explain. Just let me get to that point. The building that burnt all those years ago, Brock? It was arson. What never came out was that there was a body found. The officer who was the investigated had been first on the scene and moved it, hiding it until he could dispose of it. He has been spoken with and confirmed that. He has been arrested.

"The man who owned it? Sal Slater also owned the Slate building. That was buried in shell companies and numbered companies. We were finally able to determine that. The councilman who you suspected, Brock? His third cousin. They hid that relationship. Sal put up the money for him for considerations."

"We always wondered how he managed to get the contracts for printing and publicity that he got. He shouldn't have." Brock shared a look with Beck and then Bruce. "It was all a cover, wasn't it?"

"It was. He was involved in counterfeiting. The man who was killed? An employee of his legitimate business who found out and threatened to go to the authorities. If he had just gone and not said anything, he would be alive today. Murder has been added to the charges that Sal is facing.

"The Slate house was to have been demolished but appeals kept that from happening. We have determined that Sal was buying off clerks at city hall for one place. Everyone that he bribed has been arrested. He is facing a lot of charges."

"Now, as to you, Deri. Why did you face what you did when you returned? Sal saw you that day, decided that you had overheard his threats to the employee, and was determined that somehow you would be removed. You removed yourself when you moved to London. He felt safe when you were there but kept watch on you if he knew you were back in town.

"The woman who looked like you? She had had plastic surgery to do that. A rival counterfeiter had

238

determined what had happened, knew from Sal's drunken ramblings one night that he suspected you, and decided to play with his mind by bringing in someone who looked like you. It worked too well, unfortunately. Sal has admitted that he had you abducted, took your car, and gave it to her. He then had her killed, thinking that he had killed you.

"This last abduction? Sal had decided that you knew something, had papers that proved it. The papers? That was the book your father had been given. It has been carefully gone through and deciphered. Sal was not the one who gave it to your father, although that was how it was presented. We have determined that it was the employee who was killed who had. That will come out in court how we did that."

Davy paused for a moment. This is the hard part, isn't it, Lord? Please, let my words reflect my communion with You.

"Deri? Sal has confirmed that he was planning on taking you out of the country, to be used against your father. He would return you, unharmed, if your father agreed to never question or go to the authorities about what he suspected. That had been his plan in the first abduction, only they couldn't find out any information from you. It was the abductors who set the bomb, not on Sal's orders. We have those men in custody.

"Dallas, you were taken to use against Deri, to make her cooperate with them. Only neither one of you did. I'm sorry that we couldn't find you sooner."

Dallas shrugged. "That's life, Davy. You did what you could. God had us in His hands. It was His timing. Not ours."

"I think you have pretty much covered everything that you can, Davy. Other than what comes out in court." Will finally spoke. "I can only say how sorry I am, Deri and Dallas, that you had to go through this. Your siblings are back home. They had been threatened by Sal and we stashed them where they were safe. I would hazard a guess that they'll be heading this way in the next few days."

Dallas grinned. "They are on their way already. Sean thinks that they'll hit town late tonight. Susan was grumbling at them."

A month later, Dallas stood in his home office doorway, watching as Deri worked away sorting out his books and hers. She hummed softly to herself before she sensed that she was not alone. A glad smile lit up her face as she sprang towards him, to be caught into his arms and close to his heart.

"Have a good day, love?" He stared down at her beloved face, a smile on his as he felt her toes digging into the tops of his feet.

"I did. I spoke with that musician and we are working on more songs for her. Elizabeth is to call in the morning." She tilted her head back. "How about you?"

"I did. I started our first investigation. It will be a challenge but God is there." He turned her to face the room. "I like what you're doing in here. Extra books?"

"We have some duplicates in all those. I kept some of mine and some of yours. The rest? I'll donate somewhere if that works."

"It does." Dallas turned her and walked through the rest of the house, ending up in the sunroom that he had built onto the house at some point. "I see you have been at work."

The baby grand piano that had been his wedding gift to her stood near the French doors to the back yard, a pile of papers on one corner of the top.

"I have been. I am finding new inspiration every day. What we went through? That has indeed called us to return to our roots with God, to our basics in our faith. I would not have chosen that route, but God did."

"He did, love. Now, I would like to take my bride out for dinner. But only if she wants."

"She wants. Casual or dress?"

"Dress, I think." He reached for the box that he had set down on a table earlier. "A corsage for you to wear."

She opened the box, smiling down at the flowers before beaming at him. "You spoil me."

"And you deserve to be spoiled."

Later that evening, Dallas stood in his home office, staring around before he nodded. Deri had been at work in there as well. The room was large enough that it wasn't crowded even putting in a desk for her near the tall windows that overlooked the street. He could see the neat piles of papers that she had stacked there. The sound of music filled his home now, he thought. I always liked a quiet house to come home to but having Deri and her music to fill it has made it home.

Deri watched him for a moment before she approached, her arms wrapping around him.

"I spoke with Davy earlier today."

"Did you?" Dallas stared down at her before he pulled her to a seat on the couch. "What did he have to say?"

———

"Not a lot. He apologized again for not protecting us. I told him that he couldn't have. That God had us under His care."

"That He did. I was so scared that they would really hurt you."

Deri stared at the finger that had been broken. The splint was gone and she was working on strengthening it again.

"He really did protect us. I never doubted that He would. I just didn't expect it as it happened. Did I tell you that they threatened to kill you in front of me?"

"No, you didn't. You should have."

"I know." Deri sighed, her eyes on the rug at her feet. "I guess I was in shock. I know I told Davy. He says it will be months yet before we head to court."

"It will be. We'll need to keep dealing with this. How are your folks?"

"Mom was by this morning. She still looks ragged, as Dad says, but she says that they're talking to people who can help. I can't imagine how they felt."

"No, nor can I, even though I have been through it with victims and their families."

There was quiet in the room for a while before Dallas shifted and then spoke.

"Any regrets about the size of the wedding? We could have gone larger."

"No, it was just right." Deri thought back to that day just a couple of weeks prior. They had opted to have just their friends for the ceremony and reception.

They were planning an open house later, in about a month, for their church family and their friends. They had not wanted a lot of commotion, given what they had gone through.

"Dallas?" He looked down at her. "Did I tell you today how much I love you?"

"You did. And I love you too." His kiss sealed the unspoken promise that both of them spoke, that of their love for one another.

"Are we through with adventures now?" Deri knew that she sounded plaintive, but she also knew how much had been taken from Dallas over the months.

"I pray that we are, love. I pray that we are. If not, God will give us the strength to get through. I was struggling for a long time, not sure what way to turn. He called me to return to Him. Part of that call was you."

Thank you for choosing to read the story of Dallas and his love, Deri. He was only to be a minor character, a police detective, in *The Barnabas Chronicles*. In fact, he was never given a name in the stories, only known as Dallas. It was about a month or so ago I found him standing and staring at me, a smile on his face. My last name is Chisholm, he informed me. I need a lady love of my own. From that conversation that I had with him grew his story. It was not planned or at least the plans that I had were not used. Unruly characters that I have always choose to tell their own story, in their own way.

Abe and Emma and Nathaniel and Elizabeth showed up once more. Their stories are in the *His Guardians* series. I missed these eight men and their ladies when the series finished but lately, they have decided that they need to show up in others. They always bring a sense of helpfulness when they do.

And if you have read *The Barnabas Chronicles* and note that both Darbie and Burnie changed the spelling of their names? Unruly characters that they are finally decided to look at their birth certificates and realized that they had been spelling them wrong.

What does it take to return to God? An open and willing heart. A desire to walk with Him once more. A belief that He welcomes home the prodigal son or daughter. I have no doubt that He does. My father used to refer to a time away from God as wandering in the desert, just like the Israelites did. He was so wise. I miss the counsel that he would give. He was a quiet man, not one of many words, but when he spoke, it was a word that had been deeply thought through.

As we face uncertain times in 2021, look to our God. He is still there, in everything and every place. Never fear to turn to Hm.

God bless.

Ronna